Raine turned, her eyes widening.

Chase was handsome in faded jeans and dusty cowboy boots, but in a tuxedo, he could stop traffic. "Hello," she managed to say.

"Hello." His gaze swept her from head to toe, then returned with disconcerting slowness until he looked into her eyes again. The heat in his own eyes left no doubt that he liked what he saw.

Raine felt his slow survey as if he'd stroked his hand over her bare skin. Her body reacted with heat that began low in her belly, spreading quickly until she burned.

"So," she said nervously. "How does it feel to be consorting with the enemy?"

He laughed, the deep chuckle reverberating up her spine.

"Ask me again when this is over. I'll let you know."

Dear Reader,

Before I became a published author, I worked in the legal field. As I sat in courtrooms and listened to judges handing down jail sentences, I often wondered what happened to those convicted people and their families after their day in court. How did being incarcerated affect a person's character? What happened to their loved ones while they were locked away in a jail cell? And how did the experience change and shape all of their lives five, ten or fifteen years later?

Those questions and exploring possible answers became the heart of THE McCLOUDS series. Chase McCloud was changed irrevocably when he was unjustly convicted as a teenager—and the events leading to his imprisonment also changed Raine Harper's life forever. Fifteen years later, is it possible these two people can heal old hurts for both their families and forge a future together?

I hope you enjoy Chase and Raine's story, and that you'll return to Wolf Creek with me for the fourth and last installment in THE McCLOUDS OF MONTANA when Trey Harper is determined to expose long-hidden secrets and bring justice to the McClouds.

Best wishes,

Lois Faye Dyer

CHASE'S PROMISE

LOIS FAYE DYER

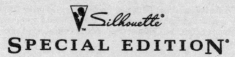

SPECIAL EDITION®

Published by Silhouette Books

America's Publisher of Contemporary Romance

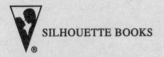

SILHOUETTE BOOKS

ISBN-13: 978-0-373-28039-1
ISBN-10:   0-373-28039-4

CHASE'S PROMISE

Books by Lois Faye Dyer

Silhouette Special Edition

Lonesome Cowboy #1038
He's Got His Daddy's Eyes #1129
The Cowboy Takes a Wife #1198
The Only Cowboy for Caitlin #1253
Cattleman's Courtship #1306
Cattleman's Bride-To-Be #1457
Practice Makes Pregnant #1569
Cattleman's Heart #1611
The Prince's Bride #1640
*Luke's Proposal #1745
*Jesse's Child #1776
*Chase's Promise #1791

*The McClouds of Montana

LOIS FAYE DYER

lives on Washington State's beautiful Puget Sound with her yellow Lab, Maggie Mae, and two eccentric cats. She loves to hear from readers and you can write to her c/o Paperbacks Plus, 1618 Bay Street, Port Orchard, WA 98366.

Chapter One

Wolf Creek, Montana
Early Spring

Chase McCloud stared at his grandfather's casket, ignoring the group of mourners huddled beneath umbrellas on the far side of the open grave. The wind picked up, carrying the scent of sage as it whipped the prairie with a flurry of icy raindrops.

His little sister shivered, clutching his

hand tighter, and he bent toward her. "Are you okay, Jessie?" he asked gently, scanning her tear-streaked face.

She nodded beneath the mop of auburn curls, but her expression was filled with fear as she darted a glance over her shoulder.

Chase squeezed her hand reassuringly.

Anger coursing through him, he knew without looking what frightened Jessie. A uniformed Montana Department of Corrections officer stood several yards behind them. The officer had removed Chase's handcuffs when they'd arrived at the cemetery and the metal restraints were clipped on the police issue leather belt, just behind his holstered gun. The officer had respected the family's grief and stood silently. Nonetheless, Chase was aware the man's attention never wavered; he swore he could almost feel the officer's searing scrutiny.

Chase focused on the mahogany casket, purposely blanking his mind to all else. Fresh grief slammed through him.

His grandfather had been a powerful, guiding influence in his life. The knowledge that Angus McCloud would no longer give him wise advice, that Chase would never again hear him laugh with delight over a new joke, was incomprehensible.

Tears burned behind his eyelids. He narrowed his eyes, forbidding the tears to fall. Raising his gaze from the casket, he turned his focus to the mourners on the far side of the grave.

His grandfather's lifelong friends and neighbors had known Chase for all of his seventeen years but now they either refused to meet his eyes or glared at him with accusation and disdain.

Clearly, few of them believed he'd been jailed unjustly.

Chase sighted the five members of the Kerrigan family. Fifteen-year-old Zach Kerrigan stood next to his mother and little sister, his stance protective. Just beyond them was Laura Kerrigan-McCloud, Angus McCloud's widow.

He still didn't understand why his grandfather had married Laura Kerrigan. They were both in their late seventies when they'd wed despite the vehement protests of both their families. The marriage appeared to bring a quiet contentment for Angus but hadn't drawn the families any closer together. The McClouds had been feuding with the Kerrigans since 1922, when a crooked poker game cost a McCloud 2500 acres of prime land. Over the years, the two families had argued and fought over a variety of grievances and there was no love lost between them—except for Angus and Laura.

Now the white-haired widow stood apart from her late husband's family, leaning heavily on the arm of her nephew, Harlan Kerrigan.

Harlan's gaze met Chase's and the older man's lip curled in a sneer. Despite the bitter rage that swelled in his chest, Chase didn't react, just looked away. Harlan's son, Lonnie hadn't come.

It's probably a good thing Lonnie's not here, Chase thought. *Granddad's funeral is hard enough on Mom and Dad. Not the place for me to meet Lonnie.*

He swept the crowd again, hoping to catch a glimpse of any members of the Harper family but none of them were at the graveside.

The stab of loss and regret was unavoidable. Chase steeled himself against letting the pain change his expression.

He and Mike Harper had been best friends since grade school and now Mike's family with no doubt believed Chase was responsible for his death. The twelve people sitting on the Wolf Creek jury certainly had—they'd convicted him of vehicular manslaughter, based on the testimony of Harlan and Lonnie Kerrigan.

I'm the only one who knows it's not true. Once again he met Harlan Kerrigan's hostile gaze. *Correction*, he thought grimly. *Both Harlan and Lonnie know who really killed Mike.*

Seething with bitterness, Chase focused on the casket once again, concentrating on breathing in and out with slow, measured inhales and exhales. He'd learned the method from a tough, no-nonsense guard at the correctional facility a week after he'd arrived at the institution. Defending himself in a brawl in the exercise yard had resulted in a six-inch knife wound and the guard had taken him to the infirmary to have the deep cut stitched. Following the guard's advice, he'd signed up for meditation classes. Combined with long hours spent weight lifting and working out, after two months he'd become strong enough to enforce his desire for solitude. As a result, the other inmates now left him alone.

Alone was just fine; being left alone was what he wanted. He planned to do his time and get out.

He drew in a deep breath, filling his lungs with cold air and the scent of sagebrush. Freedom. He craved it.

But first, he had to survive the next

few years locked away for a crime he hadn't committed.

Raine and Trey Harper lay flat on their bellies, peering around the sagebrush. From their vantage point atop the low hill, the twelve-year-olds had an unobstructed view of the Wolf Creek Cemetery and the cluster of people around the open grave.

"He looks different," Raine said. "Don't you think Chase looks different, Trey?"

Her brother stared hard at the McClouds. "He looks sad. And older. Maybe thinner. I wonder if he gets good food in jail."

"I hope so." Raine fell silent. "I miss Mike. And I miss Chase, too. I wish this year never happened."

"Well, it did." Trey didn't face her but she knew he was fighting back tears, just as she was. She always knew when her twin was upset, just as he knew things about her without asking. Their mother said twins were connected in some weird way. Raine didn't think of it as strange; for her it was normal.

"I don't believe Chase hurt Mike on purpose, do you?" she asked.

"People say he did. Mom believes he did."

"But Dad said Chase says he didn't. Do you think he did?"

"No." Trey looked at her, his gray eyes fierce. "I don't."

"Me, either." She looked away from him, back down the hill. "But he's still gone away and we never get to see him— just like Mike, only Mike's dead and Chase isn't. Do you think Chase will ever come back?"

"I don't know. Maybe someday, when I find out what really happened."

"Do you think Mom will believe you?" Raine didn't understand her mother since Mike was killed. She stayed in her bedroom, crying day and night. Sometimes it felt like she no longer even remembered Raine and Trey were in the house. It was scary and so sad it made Raine feel like crying, too.

"Probably not." Trey's voice was bleak.

Below them, the service seemed to be finished. The mourners started walking toward their cars.

Trey scooted backward. "Come on, Raine. We don't want anyone to see us. We'll be in trouble with Dad for sure if he knows we came out here."

Raine inched backward, rocks and twigs scratching her ankles where her jeans rode up above her socks. When the slope of the hill hid them from view, they stood, racing to their bikes and pedaling furiously down the little-used dirt road back to town, hurrying to get home before they were missed.

Fifteen years later
Late August

Gravel crunched under her car's wheels as Raine Harper braked, slowing to read the name printed on the mailbox atop its sturdy black metal post.

"C. McCloud," she said aloud, stopping her car and letting the engine idle.

Chase McCloud's home lay thirty miles southeast of Wolf Creek, at the farthest boundary of McCloud Enterprises land amid towering buttes and deep coulees. No fertile fields of wheat or oats softened the landscape here. Instead, barbed wire fences marched for miles along the sharply curved road, dividing the gravel highway from untamed land. Outcroppings of shale and cliffs of clay dropped precipitously to create miniature canyons where swift-running creeks sparkled in the sunlight.

Raine knew that farther south, the land grew even wilder in the Missouri Breaks. But here, blocky red-and-white Hereford cattle, horses and the occasional pair of pronghorn antelope grazed on clumps of tough grass scattered amid gray-green sagebrush.

Rumor had it that Chase McCloud had purposely chosen to live on this outer section of his family's property because he wanted to get as far away from Wolf Creek residents as possible. Raine had no idea whether the gossip was true and she couldn't afford to care.

The reclusive bounty hunter might not want visitors. He probably wouldn't welcome a Harper knocking on his door. But she needed him. She was desperate and he was the only man in the county who had experience in locating missing persons.

He owes me, she thought. *He owes my family*. She shifted the car into gear and turned off the highway onto the graveled lane.

The well-maintained road followed the bulge of a towering rocky butte. Raine rounded a curve and caught her breath, staring at the house and outbuildings tucked against the foot of a butte across the broad valley stretching in front of her. The house was a weathered A-frame with glass across the entire front. Built of peeled logs, it was surrounded by green lawn and tall maple trees. The barn,

corrals and other outbuildings were all
constructed of logs with the same aged,
silvery look.

The road cut straight across the valley.
Raine drove over a sturdy log bridge
spanning a clear-running creek then onto
the graveled drive that led to the ranch
yard. She parked in front of the house
and got out, pausing to survey the cluster
of buildings.

Very impressive, she thought, grudg-
ingly acknowledging the care and
prosperity evident in the well kept head-
quarters.

A wrought iron fence surrounded the
house and yard. The gate's latch gave
easily under her hand and she pushed it
wide, turning to fasten it behind her. Her
footsteps echoed on the wooden decking
as she approached the screened door and
rapped briskly. No one answered. The
house was silent except for the musical
tinkling of a wind chime as it swayed in
the slight breeze.

The delicate wind chime and the

scrolls of the iron fence were the only colorful touches, no pots of flowers graced the deck and the doormat was a serviceable thick brown straw.

Walking over to the edge of the deck, Raine shaded her eyes with her hand, searching the ranch yard.

All seemed quiet, the buildings and corrals drowsing in the hot sun. Her heart sank with disappointment.

He's not here.

Chase McCloud was elusive. According to rumor, he often disappeared for stretches of time, traveling back to Seattle where he'd worked as a bounty hunter for so long. He was said to still take cases for the company on occasion and to be a silent partner in the exclusive investigative agency.

Raine didn't know what she'd do if he'd left town again. Increasingly frustrated and impatient, she'd been waiting for days already. Finally Chase had returned to Wolf Creek.

She needed to see him now. She

couldn't afford to wait until tomorrow or next week.

She rapped on the door again, listening for movement inside while rubbing her knuckles.

Discouraged, she went back to her car, pausing with the door open while her gaze swept the ranch yard and buildings one last time. Just as she'd given up, the sound of a hammer ringing on metal reached her ears.

She turned, looking all around the buildings. The ring of hammer against iron sounded again, not a single blow this time but a rhythmic tapping.

As Raine headed toward the sound, she caught sight of a trace of smoke coming from the chimney atop an outbuilding beyond the barn.

She crossed the graveled ranch yard quickly, dust puffing up beneath her sandals. The nearer she drew, the louder the hammering grew. She rounded the side of the building and found long sliding doors pushed wide on their tracks, leaving the space open to the elements across one whole side. She stepped into the shadowy interior and halted, stunned.

A man, stripped to his waist, stood at an old-fashioned forge. Sweat had dampened his black hair and the heavy muscles of his upper torso gleamed, his tanned skin marked with numerous scars.

He looked up when she entered, his blue eyes narrowing as he appeared to evaluate her in one searing glance before returning his attention to the piece of red-hot metal on the anvil.

"Chase McCloud?" she asked, although she recognized the fierce blue eyes and handsome, sharp-planed features. She'd seen him a month or more earlier when she'd literally bumped into him one afternoon. On her way to talk to Trey in his apartment above the Saloon, she'd just stepped inside the bar door as Chase was leaving. Taken by surprise, he'd walked into her, grabbing her arms to keep from knocking her down. His apology for colliding with Raine had been abrupt and distracted.

She certainly remembered him but she doubted he remembered her. She knew what he'd seen in that one swift look— the same mahogany hair and gray eyes he'd been familiar with when she was a little girl and he was her oldest brother's best friend. Yet she'd caught no flicker of recognition on his face just now before he turned back to the forge.

"I'm McCloud."

"I'm Raine Harper," she began.

"I know who you are," he interrupted. "What are you doing here?" He didn't look at her, his attention focused on the hot iron, turning it as he hammered, shaping the glowing end into a long, graceful curve.

Raine tucked her fingertips into the front pockets of her jeans. "I want to hire you."

"To do what?"

"Find my brother—he disappeared over two weeks ago. I haven't heard from him and no one's seen him for seventeen days."

"Did you call the cops?"

"Yes. But they tell me they've reached a dead end. They won't resume an active search unless there are new leads to follow. That's why I want to hire you."

"No."

Raine blinked. "Why not?"

Chase tapped the hammer against the iron curve one last time and turned to thrust the metal into a barrel. The hiss of cold water meeting hot iron was accompanied by steam rolling upward. He took a ragged towel from his back pocket and rubbed his face and hair, then scrubbed it over his chest before tossing it on the bench behind him.

He picked up a black T-shirt lying next to the damp towel and pulled it over his head and arms, yanking it down as he came toward her.

Raine tensed as he approached but he simply walked past her and out into the sunlight.

"Wait!" She hurried after him. "The least you can do is give me a reason—tell me why you won't look for Trey."

"I don't want to."

His answer was so blunt it left Raine speechless for one shocked moment before a flood of anger erased caution. She grabbed his arm and he halted to look down at her. His blue eyes were remote. It wasn't so much hostility but the total lack of emotion on his face that made Raine quickly release her grip on his forearm.

"Why not?"

He didn't answer.

Frustrated, Raine frowned up at him. "My brother's missing and you're a bounty hunter. If the police can't find him, you're the only person in the area that has a chance of locating him."

"Maybe he doesn't want to be found."

"No." She shook her head, adamantly rejecting the possibility. "Trey would have told me if he were going to be gone longer than overnight. He knows I worry. He would have phoned."

"Then maybe he isn't able to make a call."

"You mean he might be dead. He's not." She saw the flicker of skepticism in his expression. "We're twins. I'd know if he were dead."

"Then why are you worried?"

"Because something's wrong. I can feel it."

"You can 'feel' your brother's in trouble? Is this some psychic thing?"

"Yes. I know it sounds weird, but we've always known if the other was in trouble, or hurt. And I know I have to find Trey. Will you help me?"

"Sorry. I never take cases from locals."

Raine clenched her fists, her temper flaring. "You owe me," she told him. "You owe my family."

His face hardened, a muscle flexing along his jawline. "I don't owe you anything, lady."

"You cost me and my family one brother when Mike died. You owe it to me to help save Trey."

"If I owed your family a debt, which I don't, I paid for it with three years of my life." His voice was as cold and hard as a Montana winter.

He spun on his heel and stalked away.

"Trey disappeared when he went to meet someone who promised to tell him the truth about the night Mike died," Raine called after him in a last, desperate bid for his cooperation.

Chase stopped walking. He turned to look at her, menace in every line of his body.

"What did you say?"

Raine felt as if she'd poked a mountain lion with a stick and had him turn on her. She'd wanted Chase's attention. Now she had it and chills of fear prickled her skin.

"Trey received a letter telling him that if he wanted to know how Mike really died fifteen years ago, he should be at the Bull 'n' Bash tavern in Billings on Friday night. He refused to let me go with him and he hasn't come home."

"Was the letter signed?"

"No."

"Have you got it?"

"No. Trey took it with him when he left for Billings."

Chase propped his hands on his hips, his expression unreadable.

"All right." He nodded abruptly. "You've got yourself a hunter. I'll need all the information you can give me about your brother. Have you got a picture with you?"

Raine was dizzy with relief. "Not with me, no. But I have several on Trey's computer in the apartment above the Saloon."

"I'll need a recent photo and his statistics, date of birth, eye and hair color, height and weight. Also what kind of car he was driving and the license number." He broke off and thought for a moment. "Has his car been found?"

"No. He drove his SUV. It's missing, too."

"Get the data together and I'll pick it up this evening on my way out of town."

"Where are you going?"

"Billings. If that's the last place he was seen, that's where I'll start looking."

Ten minutes later, after telling Chase to come to her brother's apartment above the Saloon to collect the information about Trey, Raine was racing down the highway toward Wolf Creek. She didn't have a lot of time to collect Trey's vital statistics and choose a photo of her brother to give to Chase.

For the first time in days, the heavy dread that weighed down her heart lifted, giving her hope.

Chase McCloud was more dangerous in person than his reputation claimed. Raine didn't care. She'd have dealt with the devil himself if it meant a chance to find Trey.

Chapter Two

Chase stood on his deck, watching the small red car until it turned onto the highway and sped out of sight.

Raine Harper had just knocked his world off its axis. And not only because a possible clue had surfaced in a fifteen-year-old mystery.

He hadn't lied to her—he didn't take cases for locals. He wanted nothing to do with Wolf Creek residents. He'd sworn long ago to focus on the present and let the past lie undisturbed—that included Mike's death and the local jury that held him responsible. Raine, however, was the exception.

She was the last woman he'd expected to see when he looked up from the hot metal taking shape under his hammer and saw a female form silhouetted by the sunlight. Then she'd stepped inside the workroom and he could see her clearly.

He'd recognized her with one glance.

That brief moment when they'd collided in the Saloon weeks ago was seared in his memory. He'd looked down into startled grey eyes and pink lips parted in surprise. For a second, their bodies were pressed together from chest to thigh. Those eyes, her mouth, creamy skin, mahogany hair and the feel of her curves against him had featured prominently in his dreams ever since.

He hadn't decided what, if anything, he wanted to do about her. Given their family history, he'd doubted she'd be willing to share casual conversation with him, let alone consider the kind of relationship that ended up with the two of them getting naked.

He had a strict rule against getting involved with anyone hiring his services. He'd never broken it in all his years as a bounty hunter.

Agreeing to search for her brother made Raine his client. He hoped to hell he'd be able to keep his distance until he'd located her brother and had a look at the mysterious letter.

For the first time in his life, Chase wasn't confident his control was unshakable.

Several hours later, Chase tossed a small duffel bag packed with essentials onto the floor behind the SUV's driver's seat, whistling a brief melodic tune. Three-year-old Killer, a ninety-eight pound Rottweiler, immediately ceased sniffing the grass by the house gate and trotted forward. He leaped easily into the backseat and Chase slammed the door behind him before sliding behind the wheel.

The late-afternoon sun heated the

interior of the black four-wheel-drive vehicle but Chase didn't turn on the air-conditioning, choosing instead to lower all the windows. Killer stuck his head outside, eyes half-closed as the hot wind pinned his ears back.

Chase drove by instinct, his mind occupied with the possible angles presented by the mysterious letter sent to Trey Harper just before he'd disappeared.

There were only three people who knew what really happened the night Mike Harper died. Chase was one of them. The other two were Lonnie and Harlan Kerrigan. One of them must have sent the letter to Raine's brother. But which one? And why?

Chase was convinced neither Harlan nor Lonnie would come forward and confess which meant he had to consider a third possibility. Could someone else have been present at the accident scene fifteen years earlier?

He remembered the sequence of events leading up to the crash on the highway outside Wolf Creek clearly. But he'd been thrown from the truck on impact, hit his head, and lost consciousness. Could another vehicle have arrived on the scene while he'd been comatose? Could a fourth person have seen Harlan remove Lonnie from the driver's seat and put Chase behind the wheel?

The unlikely scenario was easier to accept than the equally unlikely possibility that one of the Kerrigans had suddenly become conscience-stricken and had decided to confess after all these years.

Chase reached Wolf Creek and pulled into the alley behind the Saloon, parking several yards from the back door. Leaving Killer on guard in the SUV, he went inside. A stairwell rose to his immediate right and he moved silently up the steps to the second floor where two doors, directly opposite each other, opened off the carpeted landing. He knocked on 2B and waited, rewarded moments later by the snick of a dead bolt as it slid free.

Raine stood in the doorway. Chase stilled, rocked by the sudden urge to reach out, catch her narrow waist and draw her close. He felt an intense, nearly compulsive desire to bury his face against the thick mahogany fall of hair, wind the long strands around his fists and run his tongue over the lush fullness of her lower lip to discover the taste of her mouth.

He never broke his strict rule against romantic involvement with a client, no matter how beautiful. Raine Harper was off-limits.

He made his response as impersonal as possible. "Evening."

"Come in," she said, her gray eyes meeting his. "Is something wrong?"

"Not that I know of, why?"

"I'm not sure," she said slowly. "For a moment there, you seemed angry."

He shrugged and didn't answer her.

"Well…" She gestured him inside. "I'm just printing out a digital photo and the details about Trey you wanted."

Chase stepped past her and into the apartment. Raine went over to a desk tucked beneath a window to their left. As she moved past him, the subtle scent of her perfume reached his nostrils and he tensed, edgy and restless until she was beyond his reach.

He glanced around the apartment. Nearly half of the square footage was open space with high ceilings and polished wood floors. A kitchen took up one corner, separated from the great room by a bar with four stools. Shining copper pans hung from a rack above the stove.

Everything he'd heard about the two surviving members of the Harper family indicated that Raine and Trey were successful businesspeople. They owned the Saloon with its adjoining restaurant, the motel on the edge of town and a small apartment building a few blocks away.

Which left very little time for cooking, he thought.

The soft click and whir of a computer

printer was the only sound in the quiet apartment. "Nearly finished, only one more page to go. It took longer than I'd hoped to find the information you wanted. I'm not used to Trey's computer programs."

"This is your brother's apartment?"

"Yes. He likes the convenience of living above the business—says he spends so much time at work it's a waste of time to keep a home somewhere else." She had her back to him as she leaned forward to slip the last sheet from the printer and paper-clipped it together with several others. "I didn't ask you how much you charge for your services."

She looked over her shoulder at him.

Her eyes widened when Chase quoted his daily fee. "Plus expenses," he added.

She stared at him for a moment before nodding and turning back to the desk.

She barely flinched, he thought, which confirmed his earlier guess that the family businesses were doing well.

Chase's gaze flicked idly over the

room. A medium-size duffel bag, bulging with its contents, sat on the floor next to the door. A woman's purse sat beside it.

"Going somewhere?"

"Yes."

The timing was too coincidental. Chase instinctively knew the answer but he asked the question anyway, hoping he was wrong. "Mind if I ask you where?"

"Not at all. I'm going with you. Or I'm following you, take your pick."

"This isn't a pleasure trip. It's business and I work alone."

"You need me." Her voice as stubborn as the set of her chin, she turned to him in profile as she slipped the sheaf of papers into a file folder.

"For what?" He didn't bother hiding the sarcasm in his response.

"Psychic connections between twins have been documented and scientifically accepted. If Trey is near, I'll feel him. Without me, you could walk within three feet of him and never know it."

"And if he's dead?"

A shudder shook her slim body before she visibly collected herself. "He isn't. I would have felt him leave me."

Chase didn't believe her but it didn't take a genius to see she was fully convinced she was right. Nevertheless, he'd signed on to locate her missing brother; it wasn't his job to make her face reality. *Unless I have to tell her I've found a dead body*, he thought grimly. "It sounds like a lot of psychobabble to me but I've heard stranger things." He shrugged and held out his hand. "I'll take the photos and any information you've got on your brother."

Raine handed him the folder and he flipped through it, scanning the pages.

"Looks like enough to start with." He went toward the door.

"Are you going to let me ride with you? Or are you going to insist I drive my own car?"

He looked back at her. "You can come with me." Her taut expression eased. "Don't think it's because I want you along or agree your help is necessary," he said bluntly. "I'm saying yes because I figure it's the quickest way to convince you to stay home and let me get on with my job. Clients generally believe hunting people is either easy or exciting—it isn't. It's mostly boring, repetitive work with endless knocking on doors and conversations that lead to dead ends."

She flushed and nodded, her eyes snapping with anger, her lips set tightly.

Chase guessed her pretty mouth was clamped shut to keep from telling him exactly where he could put his ultimatums but he didn't care. He'd long ago run out of the patience required to deal with civilians who believed the television version of "bounty hunting." He was good at his job, and sometimes it *was* exciting and definitely dangerous. Most of the time, though, it required methodical, patient sifting of information.

She'll be bored and heading for home within forty-eight hours, he thought.

Raine snatched up her bag and purse and

followed him out of the apartment, pausing to lock the dead bolt. *He couldn't have been clearer about not wanting me with him.* She wondered if he'd go out of his way to be difficult and steeled herself for an unpleasant drive. If she was lucky, she thought, they'd learn something definitive in Billings and she wouldn't have to be in his company for more than the evening.

Chase had already disappeared into the alley when she reached the bottom of the stairs. A black SUV was parked a few feet away, the tinted windows adding a secretive air to its sleek appearance.

"Give me your bag. I'll put it in the back."

Raine jumped. Chase moved so quickly she hadn't heard him approach. He took the duffel from her and opened the passenger door, waving her in. Raine slipped into the seat and twisted to fasten her seat belt while Chase walked around the back of the vehicle.

Someone breathed loudly in her ear,

the sound faintly threatening. Raine glanced over her shoulder and directly into the face of a huge black dog. She froze, afraid to move. His mouth was open, red tongue lolling, and his white incisors appeared razor sharp.

"Killer. Down." Chase's voice was calm, commanding.

The big dog sat back on his haunches, giving a low growl as Chase tossed Raine's duffel on the floor at his feet. Seconds later, Chase slid behind the wheel next to Raine. The engine turned over with a throaty roar and he drove out of the alleyway.

Raine took measured breaths to slow her racing heart.

"He's…big, isn't he?"

She felt the scrutiny of Chase's gaze as he looked briefly at her before returning his attention to the highway. "Not so big for a Rottweiler. He weighs around a hundred pounds."

Raine felt her eyes widen but she didn't comment. The dog was within twenty pounds of her own weight. She hoped he wasn't easily provoked. "Is that why you named him Killer?"

"Not me—Dad named him 'Killer' after Jerry Lee Lewis, a badass fifties rock 'n' roll singer. My parents have a male Rottweiler—Killer's one of his off-spring. The elderly neighbor that raised Killer from a pup died last month and Dad took him back."

"How did he end up living with you?" Raine was fascinated by the small window into the lives of the McCloud family.

"His choice—not mine. I had dinner with my folks a few days after Dad picked him up and Killer jumped into my truck bed. He wouldn't get out so I took him home with me. He's been there ever since."

"He adopted you?"

Chase shrugged. "Apparently."

"Brave dog," she commented.

"Not really. Have you seen the size of his jaws and teeth?" Chase said dryly. "I'm not about to tell him he has to go back to Dad's."

His wry humor caught Raine off guard, startling her into laughter.

Chase glanced sideways at her. "Tell me about your brother." He switched off the radio, cutting off Mick Jagger in midlyric. The silence that filled the vehicle was suddenly loaded with intimacy.

"What do you want to know?"

"Everything you can tell me. The more I know about him, the easier it will be to second-guess his actions. Start with his work schedule. You said he lives above the Saloon because of the long hours he works. Did he have any trouble with a customer lately that was out of the ordinary?"

"Not that I know of." Raine paused, mentally considering her conversations with Trey over the last weeks before he disappeared. She couldn't think of any comments he'd made about customer interaction that went beyond the usual complaints. "Most of the clientele in the Saloon and restaurant are regulars and local. Every now and then someone starts a fight but Trey hadn't mentioned any specific problems."

"Exactly what does he do at work?"

"Everything—he's completely in charge of managing the Saloon and I'm responsible for the restaurant, although we substitute for each other if needed. Trey fills in behind the bar on occasion, deals with the Liquor Board, acts as bouncer if anyone gets too rowdy, hires and fires employees—everything required of the owner."

"Has he fired anyone recently?"

Raine shook her head. "No."

"What about at the restaurant? Any disgruntled ex-employees holding a grudge?"

"Not that I'm aware of. We're a family-run business in a small town, which means most of our employees have been with us for a long time. There's always some turnover during the year but we haven't fired or hired anyone for months." She paused, trying to remember any incident with an unhappy employee. "I can't recall any recent problems with employees beyond the usual small issues like scheduling or pay raises."

"What about his personal life? Any girlfriends with unhappy ex-boy-friends?"

"If there are, I haven't heard about it. Trey has a lot of women friends but as far as I know, he's never been serious about any one of them."

"Maybe one of them wanted more than friendship."

"Maybe." Raine searched Chase's profile but couldn't read his thoughts. "Do you think Trey's disappearance is connected to his personal life in some way and not to whoever wrote the letter?"

Chase shrugged. "I'm giving equal weight to any theory. When someone goes missing, it's often connected to a personal issue."

He continued to ask questions about Trey. The time seemed to fly and Raine was surprised when the lights of Billings appeared. Chase drove down a side street and angled the SUV into a parking slot a half block away from the neon sign spelling out Bull 'n' Bash.

Raine looked up and down the street, noting the rough neighborhood. "Charming place," she said dryly.

"Oh, yeah." Chase leaned sideways and opened the glove compartment.

His shoulder pressed briefly against hers and the space was suddenly too small. Raine sucked in a breath and pressed her spine against the seat in a vain effort to distance herself but it wasn't enough. Her lungs filled with the faint scent of aftershave and soap and she felt vaguely threatened by his size and sheer presence, though he didn't say a word or look at her.

He removed a handgun from the compartment and shifted back into the driver's seat.

Unnerved, Raine watched as he checked it efficiently, then tucked it into a shoulder holster beneath his denim Levi's jacket.

"Do you expect trouble?"

He glanced at her and she felt that electric shiver of wary awareness once more. "I always expect trouble." He got out.

Raine unlatched her seat belt and followed him, determined not to be left behind.

"Stay, Killer. Watch." The murmured words reached Raine clearly before Chase stepped up on the curb. He waited for Raine to join him then led the way to the bar's entryway, where he stopped her with a hand on her forearm.

"You can go inside with me on two conditions."

"What are they?"

"I do all the talking. You're an observer, nothing more."

Her first response was to refuse. She wanted to ask questions—someone inside might have seen Trey. If they were going to find a clue that would lead them to him, this might be their best, maybe their only, chance. But Chase was the expert in this search and she didn't want to hamper any progress he might make. She nodded reluctantly. "Agreed. What's the second condition?"

"You stick to me like glue. While we're in there—" he pointed to the Bull 'n' Bash "—you pretend you belong to me. I've been here before—this isn't the local Saloon in Wolf Creek where everyone knows you and they're all your friends."

"I'm not completely naive. I've been in a few rough bars before."

"Then you know what could happen if the men think you're available. I don't want to waste time cracking some cowboy's skull because he takes a fancy to you and won't let go."

Raine stepped over the threshold. She hadn't lied to Chase. She'd been inside rough places with Trey when he'd considered expanding the family bar ownership to outlying towns. The Bull 'n' Bash was seedier than others she'd seen, but the landscape was familiar.

The jukebox on her left was playing Johnny Cash's "Walk the Line" and the crack of cue sticks against pool balls in the back of the low ceilinged room was barely audible over the heavy bass in the music. Cheap hanging lanterns gave off low-wattage light, dimly illuminating the big room with its round tables and battered wooden chairs. Several booths lined one wall and a long bar boasted worn red vinyl stools, nearly all of them occupied by cowboys of various ages and sizes.

"Let's find a booth." Chase slung his arm around her and they threaded their way around tables.

She felt surrounded by him, his arm heavy across her shoulders, his hip and muscled thigh brushing against hers as they walked. Her body felt charged with awareness and she was relieved when they reached the booth so that she could slip out from under his arm and drop onto the bench. Instead of taking the bench opposite the scarred tabletop, Chase sat down beside her, his shoulder nudging hers. Quickly, she slid along the seat into the corner. He followed her.

"What are you doing?" she hissed, taken aback at the press of his arm and the length of his thigh against hers.

He bent his head, his lips brushing against her ear. "Marking you."

Incensed, Raine met his gaze. His blue eyes were impassive, watchful. Determined not to let him see he'd shaken her composure, she merely nodded. "Of course. I should have realized."

His mouth quirked and amusement lit his eyes for a brief moment. Then he looked away from her and lifted his hand to beckon the waitress.

The strawberry blonde who answered his gesture carried an empty tray and wore skintight jeans, her curly mass of red-gold hair brushing the straps of her bright pink halter top.

"Hi, honey, what can I get you?"

"A couple of longnecks." Chase's voice was a lazy, sexy drawl.

Raine realized with a start that he was smiling at the waitress. The smile changed his features from handsome to drop-dead sexy. The waitress clearly thought so, too. Her eyes lit and she bent forward slightly, allowing the neckline of her low-cut knit top to fall forward.

"Is that all you need, honey?"

Her suggestive question had Raine bristling. The surprising reaction was unexpected, unwelcome and annoying. Neither the waitress nor Chase appeared to remember she was present and the rudeness irked her.

"For the moment."

The blonde gave him a knowing smile and sashayed her way back to the bar.

"What was that all about?" Raine whispered.

Chase turned his head to look at Raine. His expression held none of the seductive teasing he'd shown the waitress. "It's about being nice to the employees. If

Trey was in here on a Friday night, she wouldn't have missed him."

"Assuming she was working that Friday."

Chase nodded. "A pretty safe assumption since Friday and Saturday nights are the busiest nights in a bar. There's a good chance she worked the weekend shift, don't you think?"

"True." Raine knew the Saloon's employees worked at full staff on Friday and Saturday nights. "Good call," she conceded reluctantly.

The waitress came back with two frosty bottles of beer.

"Here you go," she said.

Chase handed her a twenty-dollar bill. "Keep the change."

"Thanks." She tucked the bill into the pocket of her skintight jeans.

"There is something you might help with," Chase said, returning her smile.

"What's that?" The pure speculation in her voice clearly said she was hoping for a more personal request.

Chase reached into his inside jacket pocket and drew out the photo of Trey. "I'm looking for a friend of mine. He was in here on a Friday night a couple of weeks ago."

The blonde took the photo, studied it, then held it out to Chase. "No, haven't seen him."

"Are you sure? Take another look."

She stared at the photo once again, a frown growing between her brows. Then she shook her head. "Sorry, mister. I told the cops the same thing when they asked about him a week or so ago. I've never seen this guy before."

"Were you working that night?" Chase took the photo from her outstretched hand, tucking it back inside his jacket pocket.

"I work every Friday night, Saturday, too. Tips are better on the weekend."

"Who else works weekends? Any chance one of the other waitresses waited on him and you didn't see him?"

The blonde laughed, a throaty chortle.

"Mister, there's no chance I'd have missed him." She gestured at Chase's jacket, where the photo lay hidden. "Most of our customers are regulars. Your friend is fine-looking—I'd definitely remember him if he'd come in. He wasn't here on a Friday night. In fact, I don't think he's ever been in here, at least not when I've been working and I work six shifts a week."

"Then I guess I must have misunderstood—maybe he told me he was at another bar in Billings. Are there two bars in town with the same name?"

"No." She shook her head. "There's only one Bull 'n' Bash and God knows, one's enough." The bartender roared her name and she glanced over her shoulder. "Gotta get back to work. Let me know if you have any more…questions." She winked at Chase, ignored Raine and strutted away across the room.

Chase lifted his bottle and drank, his gaze sweeping the room and its occupants. Beside him, Raine swiveled her bottle in a slow circle on the tabletop, her fingers trembling.

"He wasn't here." She felt numb with disappointment, only now realizing how desperately she'd been counting on Chase uncovering a lead tonight. "The police said they couldn't find any evidence he'd been in Billings that night but I didn't believe it. I was so sure he must have met the letter writer here and left with him."

"Before we check this place off our list, I'm going to show Trey's picture to a few more people." Chase slid out of the booth. "I'll be back in a few minutes."

He strolled across the room and joined the group of men leaning against the wall to watch the pool shooters. Raine saw him exchange words with a cowboy on his left, then he showed him Trey's photo.

She took a sip of beer, swallowed and shuddered. She didn't like beer and if she hadn't been so intent on Chase and the response of the men now looking at

Trey's photo, she wouldn't have lifted the bottle and drank.

"It can't taste that bad." A cowboy slid into the booth opposite her, grinning as he nodded at the bottle in front of her. "But since it apparently does, how about letting me buy you something better. A shot of Jose Cuervo, maybe?"

"Thanks, but no thanks." Raine nearly groaned when she met Chase's gaze across the room and registered the grim set of his mouth as he started toward her. "I have a personal rule against letting strange men buy me drinks."

"I'm not a strange man, honey. I could get downright friendly if you're willing."

"She's not."

Both Raine and the cowboy looked up. Raine's stomach lurched. Though Chase didn't move, he emanated a lethal threat that stole Raine's breath.

The young cowboy eased out of the booth, mumbled an apology and headed quickly over to the bar.

"Let's go."

Raine slid out of the booth, her body brushing Chase's as she moved past him. Heat bloomed everywhere they touched, prickling her skin and setting off warning signals. She knew he was dangerous. She'd known before she'd asked for his help in finding Trey that he would probably be difficult to work with. She'd never expected to be physically attracted to him.

She walked ahead of him across the room, aware of him following her.

They stepped out into the night.

"Did any of the men around the pool tables remember seeing Trey?" Raine asked.

"No." Chase took her arm and guided her down the sidewalk toward his SUV.

"Then he wasn't here?"

"Hard to say. I don't think he was inside the bar but it's possible the letter writer approached him outside." Chase stepped off the curb, hit the control button to unlock the vehicle. "Or maybe he never made it to Billings."

Chapter Three

"But if he didn't arrive here, then where is he?" Raine heard the thread of rising panic in her voice and struggled to control the fear squeezing her chest and throat.

"That's the million-dollar question, isn't it?" Chase gently urged her into the car.

If I had a million dollars, I'd gladly give it all to know you're safe, Trey, she thought bleakly.

In the seat behind her, Killer woofed

softly when Chase pulled open the driver's door and slid behind the wheel.

"Does Trey spend much time in Billings?" Chase asked.

Raine couldn't read his expression, though his face was turned toward her.

"Off and on. He comes down for the occasional weekend when he wants a break from Wolf Creek—sometimes I ride along and go shopping, maybe catch a movie."

"What hotel do you use when you're here?"

She gave him the name.

"I know where it is." He backed out of the parking slot. "We'll check in, show the photo to the bartender at the hotel lounge, and then you can get some sleep."

"What will you be doing while I'm sleeping?" Raine asked, suspicious that he hadn't said *we* can sleep.

"I'll probably spend most of the night working on my laptop, checking whether there's been any activity connected to your brother over the last couple of weeks."

"What kind of activity?"

"Anything—if his credit cards have been used I want to know the location. And if anyone's cashed checks on his account or used his ID for any purpose, I want any information available on the user. I'll also run a scan to find out if his car's license number is on abandoned vehicle records anywhere in the U.S."

"You think he may have been robbed and his ID stolen?" Raine asked, mulling over the possibilities, trying to control the sick fear knotting her stomach.

"Maybe, maybe not. It's standard procedure to check everything."

Raine was silent, absorbing not only Chase's listing of details, but also what she felt he was omitting, maybe on purpose. If someone else were using Trey's identification, his credit cards or his checking account, or if his car had been found abandoned, what did that say about Trey's safety?

She squeezed her eyes shut, silently repeating to herself the essential truth she couldn't forget, the only thing she had to hold on to: Trey wasn't dead. He was her twin, their lives were inextricably linked together. If his soul departed this world, she'd feel his leaving as if part of herself were being ripped away.

He's alive, she told herself fiercely. And we'll find him.

The SUV slowed and she opened her eyes, startled to realize they'd reached the entrance to the Paramount Hotel. Chase took their bags and his laptop from the backseat, told Killer to heel, and handed a vehicle key to the parking attendant.

"Will they let your dog stay here?" she asked as they crossed the sidewalk to the double glass doors edged in brass.

"Oh, yeah," he drawled, a faint hint of amusement in his tone. "They like Killer."

Raine walked beside him into the hotel lobby, the Rottweiler padding behind them.

The man behind the registration counter looked up as they approached, a broad smile instantly creasing his face in welcome. "Mr. McCloud. Good to see you. And you, too, Miss Harper."

"Hello, Ken." Raine managed a smile. Ken was a longtime employee of the Paramount; he'd checked her and Trey in and out of the hotel on more than one occasion.

Chase set the two duffel bags and his laptop in its leather case on the carpet next to Killer and took out his wallet. "We need two connecting rooms."

Startled, Raine opened her mouth to object.

"Certainly, let me check availability," Ken responded before Raine could protest, his fingers moving rapidly over the computer keyboard. "I don't have two rooms together but I do have a suite on the third floor."

"We'll take it." Chase handed him a credit card and moments later, scribbled his name on the registration sheet before accepting two key cards. "Will you have the bellman take our luggage upstairs? We're going into the lounge for a nightcap."

"Certainly."

Chase slipped one of the cards into his pocket and handed the other to Raine before taking Trey's photo from his jacket and laying it on the countertop. "Have you seen this man recently? Within the last few weeks?"

Ken moved the photo closer. "This is your brother, Miss Harper...?"

"Yes." Raine nodded, her throat constricted.

He gave her a curious look before shaking his head and handing the photo back to Chase. "I'm sorry, but he hasn't stayed with us for a month or more. I believe the last time I saw him was when the two of you were in town for the Restaurant Owners' Association dinner, Miss Harper."

"That was six weeks ago," Raine commented.

"Thanks, Ken. If you see him, will you give me a call?" Chase exchanged the photo for a card.

"Will do, Mr. McCloud."

"Killer will go upstairs with the bags."

"Of course, Mr. McCloud." Ken beckoned a bellhop to transfer their bags to their suite.

Chase took a thin leather lead from his jacket pocket, snapped it onto Killer's collar and gave the leash to the bellhop. Without comment, the man took the leash, picked up the bags and headed for the elevators across the lobby.

Astounded, Raine watched the seemingly docile Killer trot by the man's side as Chase drew her toward the doors leading to the hotel lounge.

"Why do we need connecting rooms or a suite?" she whispered.

"Because I don't know how late I'll be working or how quickly I'll get answers. Depending on responses, I might need to ask you more questions about Trey as the night goes on. You might as well sleep until I have to wake you." He eyed her. "You said you wanted to help with the investigation. Have you changed your mind?"

"No, of course not," she said promptly,

privately wondering how wise it was to share a hotel suite with a man as dangerous as Chase. *Not that he'd made a single move toward her,* she thought. It was her reaction to him that bothered her. But since she didn't plan to let him know her hormones went crazy every time he got within three feet of her, she had no cause for worry.

Chase and Raine took seats at the comfortable, upscale bar. The low-backed stools were upholstered in soft black leather, the surface of the bar in front of them a polished, gleaming ebony.

"Evening, folks. What can I get you?" The bartender looked to be in his thirties and wore the hotel uniform of black slacks, white shirt and red vest.

"Scotch," Chase told him. "Raine?"

"A glass of white wine."

Chase waited until he brought their drinks before taking out Trey's photo once again. "We're looking for the lady's brother," he said. "Have you seen this man during the last few weeks?"

The bartender picked up the photo, tilting it for better light, before handing it back to Chase. "Nope, sorry."

Raine listened as Chase asked him several questions about other bartenders on the evening shift, what waitresses may have been working and if there were other staff, such as busboys, who might have been in the lounge and seen Trey. The bartender's answers didn't give her reason to be hopeful.

He moved away to serve guests farther down the bar and Chase tossed back his drink. "So much for Trey having visited the hotel lounge that night." He gestured at the untouched glass of wine in front of Raine. "Are you going to drink that?"

"What? Oh…no."

They left the lounge and crossed the elegant lobby to the elevators. Chase pushed the call button and looked down at her. "We've barely started," he said gruffly. "I didn't expect to get a solid lead tonight."

"You didn't?" Surprised, she met his

eyes. "But I thought you felt we would learn something at the Bull 'n' Bash."

"It was an outside shot. It's the first place the police would have gone and chances were their search was thorough. The Bull 'n' Bash is a bar with a regular clientele; if Trey had been there, he would have stood out. The employees or one of the usual customers would probably have remembered him because he wasn't a regular. They would have told the cops, who in turn would have told you."

"Then why did we come here?"

"Because I never accept another professional's version of the facts."

"Ah." Raine nodded. "Being thorough and verifying reports is part of the package that results in your 98 percent success rating."

"You did your homework before you hired me."

"Of course." She eyed him. "I was hoping you'd succeeded in finding your quarry 100 percent of the time."

"Nobody in the business has a 100 percent record."

"Does anyone have a 99 percent rating?"

"Not anyone I know."

"So if Trey can be found, you're the man most likely to find him." It wasn't a question. In fact, Raine realized she was stating her own conviction and hope aloud.

He didn't reply, merely shrugged.

The elevator chimed and the doors whisked open. A group of five men in business suits, intent on their conversation, left the elevator.

Beside her, Raine felt Chase go suddenly still. She stared up at him and was surprised to see cold menace on his features, his gaze focused intently on the group.

She looked at the men, her swift intake of breath a mere whisper as she recognized Harlan Kerrigan.

A distinguished, silver-haired man was the last to exit the elevator. Deep in conversation with Harlan, he walked past them before he stopped abruptly. Recognition lit his features and he grinned broadly.

"Chase." He spun on his heel. "Good to see you. How's your dad?"

"He's well, Senator Harris. Busy as always," Chase replied, shaking the man's outstretched hand.

"That's our John. I keep telling him he needs a vacation now and then. He should take that pretty mother of yours to Mexico and soak up some sun." He laughed and looked expectantly at Raine.

"Senator, I'd like you to meet Raine Harper. Raine, this is Senator Bill Harris."

"It's a pleasure to meet you, Senator." Raine held out her hand and smiled. Her gaze didn't stray to Harlan, standing silently just beyond the senator.

"The pleasure's all mine, Miss Harper." The senator smiled benignly. "Your name seems familiar…?"

"Raine and her brother own several businesses in Wolf Creek," Chase told him.

"Ah, yes, of course. My wife and I stayed at the Harper Hotel last summer."

"I hope you enjoyed your time with us," Raine replied.

"We did. I was impressed with the friendliness of the staff," the senator said. "Well, I'd better let you two go." He looked at Harlan. "I'm holding up a business meeting."

Harlan managed a polite smile for the senator, however his expression held barely concealed dislike as he swept Chase and Raine with an assessing, cold stare.

Raine's scalp prickled. She felt an urge to step back out of the line of fire. But the senator merely lifted an eyebrow at Chase, nodded slightly in what appeared to be an acknowledgment of some sort and drew Harlan away.

Chase appeared to dismiss the incident; he pushed the elevator call button again. The doors sprang open immediately and he took Raine's arm, ushering her inside.

The doors slid shut, cutting off their view of the lobby just as Harlan and the senator disappeared through the archway into the restaurant.

"Well, that was interesting," Raine said, unable to let the matter drop.

Chase looked directly at her, and she had to steel herself to keep from retreating before the anger in the fierce, bright blue eyes. "What?" he said, the very softness and lack of inflection in his voice a threat.

"You and Harlan Kerrigan." Raine cocked her head to one side, eyeing him. "You reminded me of two heavyweight boxers being weighed in on ESPN before the big fight. The air practically crackled with hostility. I expected the two of you to take a swing at each other any minute."

"Boxers?" He seemed taken aback. "What do you know about boxers psyching each other out before a fight?"

"My dad was a boxing fan," she explained, pleased to have surprised him. "I grew up watching film clips of Smokin' Joe Frazier and Cassius Clay, before he renamed himself Muhammad Ali. Let's

see, who else? Oh, yes. Mike Tyson. Dad
wasn't a big fan of Tyson, though."

"I remember watching fights with your
dad," Chase said, a faint smile brighten-
ing his somber features. "But I don't
recall you being there."

"I didn't start watching boxing with
him until after Mike died," Raine said.
She used her brother's name purposely,
intent on reading Chase's features as he
registered her remark.

His face went blank.

The elevator pinged a warning and the
doors whisked open.

"This is our floor," Chase said.

She didn't miss the fact that he hadn't
responded when she'd brought up Mike.
Interesting, she thought. She'd always
wondered how Chase felt about Mike's
death. Had he grieved the loss of his best
friend? Did he still? Or did he resent and
blame Mike for the years he had spent in
jail after Mike died?

She was no nearer to the answer now
than she'd been fifteen years ago. And

she still wanted to know, needed to know if the boy she'd adored as a little girl still existed, deep inside the complicated, dangerous man walking by her side.

Chapter Four

Chase didn't wake Raine during the night. His computer search turned up nothing of interest on Trey Harper—no activity on his credit card or bank accounts and no new information on the whereabouts of his vehicle. Chase sent an e-mail to Ren Colter at the Seattle office of Colter & McCloud Investigations and asked his partner to run national searches for Trey through the usual resources. Finally, at 2:00 a.m., he shut down his laptop and went to bed. Given the nature of his job, he'd developed the ability to fall asleep instantly and wake just as quickly but tonight, thoughts of Raine kept him awake.

He remembered the little girl she'd once been. He was five years older than her and Trey but the much younger twins had followed him and Mike on occasion, wanting to join in their adventures. One hot summer day, Raine had fallen out of a tree house they'd built in Mike's backyard and broken her arm; afterward, Mr. Harper and his own dad had lectured them at length about looking after her and Trey. When her exasperated mother had caught Raine trying to climb the tree with her arm in a cast, Chase and Mike had dismantled the aerie and built one in the McCloud yard.

It was hard to equate the adult Raine with that little girl. Except for the dark hair and the gray eyes with their thick black lashes, nothing about her was familiar. Those gray eyes held a woman's secrets, the dark brown hair a sexy, sleek fall that called attention to the delicate shells of her ears and shape of her face. High cheekbones framed the classic line of her small nose and the lush fullness of her mouth. Raine's very adult, very feminine curves and long legs were nothing like the angular body and coltish limbs of the child that had tagged after her brothers and Chase.

He wasn't sure he totally believed she had a psychic connection to her twin but whether he believed her or not didn't matter. He'd find Trey Harper, alive or dead. And if he was lucky, the search for Trey would lead him to the person who'd written the letter. If someone was stirring up interest in a fifteen-year-old mystery, Chase wanted to know what they knew. That was his real goal.

More importantly, he wanted to know why the letter writer had kept silent for fifteen long years. On the day he was released, he'd walked away from the youth correctional facility and put the unwelcome memories behind him, vowing not to waste his life seeking vengeance against the Kerrigans. But the possibility that evidence might exist to prove his innocence in that long-ago crime was too important to ignore.

In the meantime, he needed to keep his hands off Raine.

He shouldn't have tucked her under his arm when they walked into the Bull 'n' Bash. Now he knew what the curve of her breast felt like pressed against his side, how the slide of her jeans-covered thigh against his made him ache to know what it would be like without cloth between them, and just how soft the sensitive skin below her ear was.

Dumb move, McCloud.

Something had compelled him to warn off the other men in the bar. He hadn't lived like a monk over the years—he'd had his share of women. None of them had ever made him want to claim them. It was annoying as hell that he'd been unable to ignore the urge with Raine.

He fell asleep with the memory of the scent of her hair in his nostrils and the taste of her skin on his lips.

They left Billings shortly after lunch the following day.

"Not a single person we talked to remembered seeing Trey," Raine said, dejected.

Chase glanced at her, then back at the road. She wore khaki shorts that left the sleek curves of her tanned legs bare from midthigh to her pink-tipped toes in flat sandals. A tailored shirt that looked as if she might have stolen it from her brother's closet hung unbuttoned over a white tank top and her thick mane of silky hair was pulled high off her nape in a ponytail. Her soft mouth had a downward curve and her body slumped against the leather-covered seat. They'd spent the morning walking the streets surrounding the Bull 'n' Bash, showing Trey's photo to business owners and shoppers. Unfortunately, no one recognized him.

"Investigations aren't connect-the-dots," he said. "It would have been nice to get a lead, but I'm not surprised we didn't."

"So, now what?" Raine lifted her travel mug and sipped coffee.

"Now we trace the most logical route Trey might have taken when he left Wolf Creek for Billings. There's a map in the glove compartment." He hoped giving her something specific to do would bring back that stubborn optimism he'd seen from the first moment she'd walked into his forge at the ranch.

Raine settled her mug in the cup holder and leaned forward to take out the map. The folded paper rattled as she spread it out on her lap, then refolded it to reveal the area surrounding the highway they traveled.

"This is a lot of territory." She traced the blue highway line with her fingertip. "He could be anywhere."

"He could," Chase agreed. "But we know he left Wolf Creek, which gives us a starting point. We also know he told you he planned to drive to Billings. That gives us a destination. The shortest route between the two towns is the road we're on and if he stopped for gas, coffee or food along the way, maybe someone will remember seeing him."

Raine sat a bit straighter in her seat. "Right." She scanned the map. "There's a truck stop about twenty miles ahead."

"We'll stop there for lunch, show Trey's picture around and talk with the employees to find out if anyone remembers seeing him."

"And if no one does, then we move on to the next place on the map?"

"Yes."

"This could take forever," she murmured, sounding discouraged.

"It might take a while," he admitted. "Ready to go home yet?" He realized with surprise he hoped she'd answer no. He'd never liked traveling with a client—they inevitably distracted him from the job. And Raine sure as hell was a distraction. So why did he want her here?

"No." She eyed him curiously. "What made you ask?"

Chase shrugged. "Just wondering if you'd had enough. Most clients don't make it past the first day."

"I'm guessing you were hoping I wouldn't, either," she said dryly.

"Well now, that's the thing," he drawled. "All clients are distractions that get in the way of my doing the job. You, on the other hand, are closer to what I'd call an attractive nuisance."

"Really?" she said, sounding amused.

"Oh, yeah." He glanced at her, smiling slightly at the skepticism in her eyes. "Your legs are lots easier on the eyes than my last client's—he had knobby knees and lots of red hair. I know this because we were in Mexico and he was wearing shorts. Not to mention," he continued over her laugh, "he smelled like he'd skipped soap and bathed in cheap after-shave. Gave me a headache. You, on the other hand, smell like some kind of flowers."

"And the flowers aren't giving you a headache?"

"Nope. Not yet," he responded, satisfied his teasing seemed to have made her forget her despondency over the lack of clues about her brother.

"You know," she said thoughtfully, "this is the first time I've seen you really smile. I thought perhaps you'd lost your sense of humor after all those years of chasing criminals."

"I have a sense of humor," he protested mildly.

"I haven't heard you laugh very often."

"Maybe not," he said, realizing he'd dropped his guard with her—something he normally only did around his family.

She sipped her coffee, watching the sagebrush-dotted landscape go by.

"What were you making the day I came out to your ranch and you were working at the forge?" She asked idly.

"An iron gate."

She shifted in her seat so she could watch him. "Really? For your ranch?"

"Not this time. It's a commission for a tech-millionaire in Seattle."

"I didn't know you were an artist."

"I'm not. I'm a welder, sometimes a farrier, and sometimes I make ironwork lace for fences, gates, that sort of thing."

"How long have you been doing ironwork?"

"Since I was a teenager." He glanced at her, a self-derisive smile twisting his lips. "In addition to regular high school classes, I could take career accounting or welding when I was incarcerated. I chose welding. It got me out of the classroom."

She didn't look away from his eyes. "Good choice," she said calmly. "Did you make the wind chime hanging outside the door at your house?"

He nodded. "I don't usually do small pieces but my mother wanted a wind chime. The one you saw was practice for the one I finished for her."

"It's beautiful. Call it what you like, the chime has 'artist' written all over it."

"Thanks." He knew his work was good

but it warmed something deep inside him to know she admired one of his pieces.

It surprised him that he cared she'd noticed the delicate metalwork in the wind chime. He wondered briefly if spending time with Raine was more dangerous than he knew. But before he could work out just why that might be, she asked him a question about how he'd met the tech-millionaire in Seattle who'd commissioned the iron lace fence.

Miles flew by as they drifted casually from subject to subject, Chase gaining insight into Raine's life in bits and pieces. She and Trey had taken over the family businesses while they were still in high school. Which explained why she appeared to have the maturity of a woman older than her twenty-seven years, he thought.

They reached the truck stop but their questioning of the employees there netted zero results.

By the time they reached their third stop on the map, a small ranching town just off the highway, Raine had a growing conviction that whatever had happened to Trey had occurred closer to home. None of the places they'd been to in Billings and none of the stops they'd made along the highway made her feel Trey had been there recently.

"There's a small mom-and-pop grocery store on the main street," she told Chase as he took the highway exit. "It has two fuel pumps out front and Trey has a habit of stopping there for gas on his way to Billings—he likes the coffee."

They drove through three residential blocks, the wide streets shaded by thick oak trees, before reaching the business district. The commercial center of town was only two blocks long and consisted of a feed store, grain elevator, a bar, a bank and the small grocery store. Several small offices with signs indicating they belonged to a doctor and a lawyer, as well as a couple of cafés were visible down side streets. The dusty main street was nearly deserted in the late-afternoon heat.

They turned into the grocery's parking lot and stopped in front of the two fuel pumps.

"I think I'll get a bottle of water," Raine said, unlatching her seat belt.

"I'll be a few minutes." Chase got out of the vehicle. "I'll let Killer sniff the grass over there first."

He stretched his arms over his head, his body no doubt cramped and tight from sitting behind the wheel, and Raine's mouth went dry. His grey T-shirt stretched tight over his chest, riding up to reveal a strip of bronzed skin between the hem and the waistband of his jeans. Powerful, sleek muscles were bisected by a faint line of silky black hair that started at his navel and disappeared beneath his belt buckle, just above his Levi's buttons.

Traveling with Chase held unforeseen land mines, she thought. He'd lowered his guard this afternoon and let her glimpse the man beneath the steely exterior. That Chase reminded her of the teenage boy she'd known as a child, but with a mature, wickedly attractive charm that made his physical appeal all the more powerful.

Shaking her head at her inability to ignore him, she tore her gaze from him and left the vehicle. Behind her, she heard Chase whistle softly, then the scrape of dog nails on blacktop as the Rottweiler jumped out of the SUV and the two headed for a strip of grass separating the parking lot from its neighbor.

The grocery's interior had uneven wooden floors that creaked gently beneath her feet. Raine recognized the owner sweeping the floor in the produce aisle before she went toward the refrigerated section in the back. She opened the cold case, relishing the rush of chilled air as she selected a bottle of water. The temperature outside was at least eighty-five degrees and the store didn't have air-conditioning. Instead, an old-fashioned swamp cooler whirred and rattled, struggling to cool and stir the warm air inside the high-ceilinged building.

The cooler seemed as old as the store. It reminded her of a building in Wolf Creek erected to house a dance hall in 1935. Now it was a Senior Citizens' Center and the participants loved the old stories and scandals connected to the building's heyday.

She found the snacks aisle and selected four candy bars, two for her and two for Chase. She had no idea if he had a sweet tooth but decided it might be polite to make a friendly gesture and offer him chocolate. He'd said she could accompany him on his search until she became bored and opted to go home. Despite his teasing earlier, she wasn't totally convinced he welcomed her presence on his search. Since she had every intention of sticking to him like glue until he located Trey, she could only hope Chase didn't lose patience and demand her departure anytime soon.

She carried the candy bars and bottle of water to the checkout counter and queued up behind two teenage girls and a middle-aged rancher wearing boots, jeans and a Stetson. The line moved swiftly, emptying the store except for Raine, and she was pocketing her change when Chase entered. He nodded at the young checkout clerk and handed him a credit card.

"I'm the black SUV at the second pump."

The clerk swiped the card and filled out the credit slip. The young man automatically compared Chase's signature with the card. His eyes widened.

"You're Chase McCloud, the bounty hunter?" His voice held a touch of awe.

"That's right." Chase's tone was perfectly civil but his reserve didn't encourage further conversation, his whole appearance remote and unapproachable.

The owner of the store, a gray-haired man wearing wire-rimmed glasses, gazed up at the clerk's question and his faded blue eyes lit with interest. Chase's response had him setting aside his broom and striding forward, his step spry.

"Mr. McCloud, I'd like to shake your hand. And I want to thank you—you located my neighbor's daughter, Lucy Mason, a couple of years back."

Chase shook the elderly man's outstretched hand. "How are Mr. and Mrs. Mason?" he asked.

"They're doing well, much better now Lucy's home, safe and sound. They were worried sick until you agreed to take their case."

"I'm glad to hear things are going well for them. They're nice people."

"Yes, they are. They've been my neighbors for twenty-five years—I couldn't ask for better ones. Lucy's a good kid, too—they didn't have a bit of trouble with her until she started hanging out with the wrong crowd. She went through counseling, like you suggested," the storekeeper added. "Seems to have done her a lot of good. Her dad told me her grades are back to normal and she's applying to colleges."

"I'm glad to hear she's doing so well," Chase said.

Raine stood silently, registering the deep appreciation and respect evident in the store owner's words and expression. Chase listened to the older man's comments with grave courtesy, patiently answering his questions about how he'd found the teenage runaway and returned her to her frantic parents.

At last, Chase took Trey's picture from his pocket. "I'm looking for a man that's disappeared. Have either of you seen him in here within the last few weeks?"

Both men studied the photo. Raine's hopes were dashed as each shook their head.

"I'd appreciate it if you'd give me a call if you do see him." Chase handed them each a business card. "He was driving a silver SUV. It's missing, too." He replaced Trey's photo with a picture of the vehicle and the vanity plate, HARPER2. "The plate is a little unusual."

The owner shook his head. "No, sorry. I wish I could help but I haven't seen either the driver or the SUV."

The younger clerk stared at the photo, his forehead furrowing. "I don't remember the man, but the SUV…I remember seeing it."

Raine caught her breath, hope soaring. "When?"

"A couple of weeks ago, just before closing. The reason I remember is the two guys in the car were jerks—hassled me about not having the brand of beer they wanted. I thought they'd had enough to drink—I almost called the cops after they left but it was late and they seemed to be driving okay when I watched them leave."

"Do you remember anything about them? Did they pay with a credit card?" Chase asked.

"No. They paid cash."

Chase asked several more questions but the clerk didn't remember anything more about the men. He said goodbye, cupping Raine's elbow in his palm to turn her toward the exit and they left the store.

"He remembers Trey's car and license plate, but not Trey." Raine buckled her seat belt and looked at Chase. "That can't be good news."

"It indicates Trey was separated from his vehicle before it reached this point." Chase drove out of the parking lot and headed toward the highway. "That's all it means." He glanced at her, his eyes unreadable. "Your ESP still tells you he's okay, right?"

Raine nodded, unable to speak for the fear clogging her throat.

"So we've learned another piece of the puzzle. Nothing's changed as far as your brother's safety."

"Right. I'll hold that thought."

She badly wanted to question him about the rest of the storekeeper's conversation and the teenager he'd located, but one look at his narrowed eyes and she decided against it.

No one recognized Trey or the picture of his vehicle at their next three stops. However, slightly different versions of the celebrity treatment accorded Chase happened as they left the café where they'd eaten dinner and at the following two places.

"My, my," she said, when they were on the road once again after asking the now familiar questions at a small gas station and mini-mart. "I didn't realize what a celebrity you are."

"I'm not."

"People seem to believe you are. I thought you told me you don't take local cases?" She caught the brief tightening of his mouth in profile.

"I don't take cases in Wolf Creek."

"Ah, I see."

"And of course you couldn't let the subject pass without commenting," he said dryly, flicking her a sideways glance.

"Of course not," she replied promptly. "I'm insatiably curious. So tell me, which do you like best—bounty hunting or searching for missing persons?"

"Sometimes one, sometimes the other."

When he didn't elaborate, she sighed. "And that means…?" she prodded.

"That means people pay me to do both. And since I'm sure you researched my credentials and reputation before you hired me, you already know my agency does both."

"I did check you out," she acknowledged. "Most of the information I found was only about the Colter & McCloud Agency. There was very little personal detail about you or your partner. And the public data I found on the cases your company handled was all about recovering criminals for a fee after they'd skipped town. That's why you're called a bounty hunter, right?"

"That's why we're called bounty hunters," he said dryly.

"So why do you look for missing persons? Is the money better?"

He laughed, a deep amused chuckle that shook her.

"No, the money isn't better, at least, not normally. Every now and then, the client is rich so I charge a little more to compensate for the poorer clients."

"That's very benevolent of you."

"Yeah, that's me, all right—Mr. Nice Guy."

"You're making light of it, but clearly, finding and returning Lucy Watson wasn't a small thing to her parents and their neighbor."

"It's never a small thing to the people on the waiting end," he said. "That's why I prefer people hunting to bounty hunting. Criminals on the run aren't happy campers when they're caught—I've been shot at, kicked, punched, raked with spurs, hit with swinging chains and bitten. It gets old fast. Missing persons aren't always glad to see you, but their families are happy, so it all evens out."

"Well, I think it's a wonderful thing to do. When a loved one goes missing, people become desperate," she said. "If you hadn't agreed to help me look for Trey, I don't know what I would have done."

"Don't get your hopes up. We haven't found him yet."

"But we will," she said with conviction. "And when we do, I'll be a very happy camper."

"Let's hope so." He gestured at the map. "What's the next stop?"

Raine picked up the map and traced their route. "Henderson, a little town about ten miles ahead."

"I remember a small motel there with decent beds. We'll spend the night and get an early start in the morning."

The sun was setting by the time they left the highway and reached Henderson. The sole motel was circa 1950s, one story, with parking slots outside the rooms. They checked in and went to their separate rooms.

Raine dropped her bag on the floor and though it was early, she climbed into bed, exhausted by the long day and her worries about Trey. When she woke two hours later night had fallen. Only a sliver of pale moon relieved the inky blackness looming beyond the circle of pink cast by the motel's neon Vacancy sign. No longer sleepy, she showered, put on shorts and a tank top, then switched on the TV.

She sat on the bed, propped against the headboard with pillows, and opened her journal to add notes detailing the day's events.

It didn't seem as if they'd progressed at all in their search, although she knew they were methodically covering the most logical route and places Trey may have stopped on that Friday night. She accepted it was necessary to eliminate all the possibilities but knowing Chase was being practical and thorough didn't help her frustration.

She wanted results. Now. She wanted to know where Trey was and if he was safe.

She dropped her head into her hands. She hated that, although her connection to Trey told her he was alive, it couldn't tell her where he was. Was he near, or far away? The only consolation was that she didn't get a sense he was injured. Still, it was frustrating to know he was out there, somewhere, and she couldn't find him.

Chapter Five

Chase phoned the sheriff's office in Wolf Creek to report the name and location of the store clerk who recalled the incident with Trey's SUV. After updating Ren in Seattle, he booted up his computer and ran his own scans for activity but once again, had no hits for information using Trey's name.

Nearly two hours later, he and Killer left his room and paused outside Raine's motel door while he debated whether to disturb her. The curtains were drawn across the wide window to the left of the door, lit by the glow of lamplight within. An hour earlier, the window had been dark and he guessed she'd fallen asleep shortly after they'd checked in. She was clearly awake now, though, since the muted sounds of a television were audible.

"Hell," he muttered. Killer chose that moment to sit, leaning heavily against his leg and looking up at him expectantly. "All right, all right," he told the dog. As long as Raine was determined to share in the search, he might as well let her join him in the routine questioning. *Ren would tell me it's part of keeping the client happy.* He rapped on the door and waited.

"Who is it?" she asked.

"Chase."

He heard the rattle of the security chain and the snick of the dead bolt sliding free before the door opened.

"Is something wrong?"

"No. The night shift clerk comes on

duty in five minutes. Killer and I are heading over to the office to show him Trey's picture and ask the usual questions. I thought you might want to come along."

She wore a pair of navy jogging shorts and a white tank top, her dark hair scooped up into a loose ponytail. Her face looked scrubbed and vulnerable, her eyelashes a black fringe framing gray eyes, her mouth soft, pink and bare beneath the muted glow of the light fixture mounted above the door.

He stuck his hands in his pockets to keep from trailing his fingers over the lower curve of her mouth and down the slim arch of her throat.

"Absolutely—let me get my shoes."

Chase and Killer waited outside the open door while she took a pair of sandals out of the duffel bag and slipped them on. She grabbed her room key off the nightstand and rejoined him.

They set off down the walkway, past the row of rooms, toward the brightly lit office.

He stopped at a soft drink machine and

shoved his hand into the front pocket of his jeans, taking out a handful of coins.

"Do you want anything?" he asked as he dropped quarters into the coin slot, then pushed the button for a Coke.

"I'd love a soda but I don't have any change—my purse is back in the room."

"No problem." He inserted more quarters and a second can of Coke rattled into the tray. He handed one to Raine and popped the tab on the second one. He paused, staring at her mouth when she took a long drink, closed her eyes and licked her lips.

"Thanks," she said appreciatively. "I'll buy next time."

"Right," he got out, his voice thick as he fought down the urge to haul her back into her room and lick that same path across her lips with his tongue. He was fast becoming damn near obsessed with finding out what she tasted like.

They reached the office and found the solitary night clerk, reading a newspaper spread out on the counter.

"Evening, folks," he said genially. "What can I do for you?"

Chase took Trey's photo from his back jeans pocket and laid it on the counter. "We're looking for a friend of ours. Do you recall seeing him within the last few weeks?"

The clerk peered inquisitively over the top of his half-glasses at them, then studied the photo. A frown creased his brow, then cleared. "Yes, I do."

Raine caught her breath and Chase gave her bare forearm a brief squeeze, warning her to remain silent and let him question the clerk.

"Do you remember when you saw him—how long ago?" he asked, feeling the tension vibrating in Raine.

"Sure I remember, it was the night the big semi turned over out on the highway." The clerk leaned forward, pointing out the window toward the clearly visible neon motel sign marking the exit. "Most excitement we've had around here in a long while. There wasn't a lot of traffic that Friday night, but what there was had to sit and wait for an hour or so, probably closer to two, until the tow trucks moved the semi out of the way." He looked at them and grinned. "Damn thing was carrying a load of chickens. Biggest mess you ever saw."

"Was our friend involved in the accident?" Chase tapped his forefinger on the photo.

"Him? Nah." The clerk shook his head. "He was stuck behind the wrecked semi when the highway patrol closed the road. There were four or five trucks and cars held up. Most of the drivers hiked over here and I gave them coffee, some of them got soda and snacks out of the machines. Your friend stayed and talked for a while, said he was on his way to Billings. Seemed worried he might miss seeing someone there, I think he had an appointment, maybe."

"Did he mention taking another route to Billings so he didn't have to wait for the road to clear?"

"No." The clerk shook his head emphatically. "He stayed here drinking coffee and shooting the breeze until the highway patrol and the tow trucks cleared the road. Then he left."

"Did you see him again? Maybe he stopped in for coffee on his way back from Billings?"

"No. But I went off duty at 6:00 a.m. You might want to ask Maria if she saw him the next day—she works the six to noon shift."

"Thanks, we'll do that. Anything else you remember about your conversation on that Friday night?"

The clerk thought a moment, then shook his head. "Can't say as I do—we didn't talk about anything important, just chatted, mostly about boxing. There's a heavyweight title match coming up next month."

"Thanks for all your help," Chase picked up the photo and tucked it back into his jeans pocket. "If you remember anything else about our friend, I'd appreciate you giving me a call." He handed the clerk a business card. "Anytime at all."

"Sure." The clerk read the card and his eyes widened. "You're Chase McCloud?"

"Yes."

"This guy you're asking about, is he wanted somewhere?" The clerk's voice was animated.

"No, he's a missing person. We're just trying to locate him, that's all."

"Oh." Disappointment was evident on the man's face.

"Thanks again," Chase said.

Raine murmured a thank-you and they left the office.

"I think he was disappointed you weren't tracking down an escaped killer," she commented in a low voice.

"Probably wanted to be able to tell his friends he faced a dangerous criminal and lived," Chase agreed with a slight grin.

Raine caught his arm, drawing him to a halt on the sidewalk several yards from the office where inside, the clerk leaned over the counter, still staring after them with blatant interest.

"So we know Trey got this far." She was clearly elated, almost bouncing as she turned to look at the dark highway beyond the motel lights. "At last, someone remembers seeing him."

"It's encouraging," Chase agreed.

"I'm too wound up to go back to my room and try to sleep." She pointed to the pool area, enclosed by a chain-link fence and deserted at this late hour. Underwater pool lights made the water glow turquoise, gently illuminating the concrete decking and vacant chairs. "Let's sit by the pool and you can tell me where we go from here."

Chase knew he should refuse. Sitting under the stars with her came perilously close to socializing and he had a hard-and-fast rule against associating with a client outside necessary business meetings. But the prospect of being with Raine, breathing in fresh, sage-scented air and surrounded by open space instead of trapped inside the four beige walls of the motel room was irresistible.

"All right."

They chose two deck chairs near the deep end of the pool. Raine dragged a third chair closer and kicked off her sandals to prop her bare feet on its nylon-web seat. Killer stretched out on the concrete decking between them and she reached down to rub his ears.

"Now that we've located someone who saw Trey that night and confirmed he was on his way to Billings, what's the next step?" she asked.

"We narrow the parameters of our field and keep searching."

"Meaning we concentrate on the road between here and Billings?"

He nodded. "In the morning, we'll talk to the day shift clerk. I'll put in a call to the highway patrol—the officer on duty at the accident scene might not remember Trey since he wasn't involved, but it's worth checking out."

"And then what?"

"Then we'll backtrack and recheck all the stops between here and Billings. And hope to hell we find someone else who remembers seeing your brother."

She was quiet for a moment, digesting his blunt answer. "This is only a small clue, isn't it? I mean, it's not as if we know what happened."

"It's not big but most investigations are solved by accumulating small bits of information. This isn't television, where the mystery is solved in sixty minutes. Real life doesn't work that way."

"But it *is* encouraging that we've found a trace of him, right?"

"Absolutely." His tone was firm and rang with conviction.

She drew a deep breath. "Okay, then… I'm going to focus on the good news and not think about how long it might take to gather the many small pieces of information that may be necessary before we find him."

"Smart woman," he said, lifting his Coke in a silent toast before drinking.

Raine idly scratched Killer behind the ears, smoothing her hand over the soft fur, while she sipped her soda and watched the stars twinkling brighter as the night deepened.

"How did you happen to choose a career as a bounty hunter?" she asked idly.

"What makes you ask?"

"I don't know." She looked over at him and found him slouched in his chair, watching her. He seemed relaxed and comfortable, legs stretched out in front of him, his head resting against the back of the deck chair. "Just wondering, I guess."

He studied her for a long moment, then looked away, his hands cupped around the soda can sitting on the hard muscles of his midriff. "I don't think I'd call it a choice. It was more a case of my needing a job and an employer with an opening."

"You must have applied for the job. Otherwise, how did the employer get your name?"

"One of the guards at the detention center recommended me."

"That was nice of him."

"Yeah, wasn't it," he said dryly. "Not a lot of employers stand in line to hire an ex-con."

"But you could have come home and worked for your dad?"

"I could have. But I didn't want to live in Wolf Creek. I wanted to see the world."

There was more to it than this, Raine could sense his underlying tension.

"But you're home now—does that mean you had enough of traveling?"

"I was tired of waking up in a long line of nondescript hotels in strange cities, chasing one more dumb-as-dirt criminal." He shrugged. "No matter what life is like at home, it's still home."

"What do you mean?"

He gestured, the movement indicating the rolling prairie and towering buttes, dark against the starlit horizon. "I missed the land," he said simply. "Cities don't smell like sage and clean air; they smell like exhaust fumes and frying hamburgers. In the end, I guess I just wanted to come home to the ranch."

"To the ranch—but not to Wolf Creek."

"Yeah."

"I don't see you around town. I was startled when I bumped into you at the Saloon that afternoon. I mean, I hadn't seen you since Mike died."

"Yeah, well..." His voice trailed off. He gazed broodingly at the dark buttes on the far horizon. "I don't spend much time in Wolf Creek."

"That's the understatement of the year," she chided. "I've never seen you in town, except for that one time. Where do you go shopping?"

"Shopping?" His expression was blank, uncomprehending.

"For groceries, Christmas gifts..." She waved a hand at his feet and long legs. "Clothes, boots...you know, shopping."

"Ah." He nodded. "Shopping." He eyed his long legs and crossed ankles with their well-worn jeans and polished black cowboy boots. "I had the boots made for me in San Antonio. In fact, I bought several pairs so I doubt I'll need new ones for a while. And clothes…" He tucked his chin to look down at the white T-shirt with a black-and-gray Colter-McCloud Investigations logo on the left side. "Probably won't need any of those too soon, either."

"Men." Raine shook her head in disbelief. "What about Christmas shopping?"

"I fly into Seattle several times a year. Our office is in a high-rise downtown. All I have to do is walk outside and within six blocks I can find nearly anything I want for Christmas gifts. What isn't there, I can get on the Internet and have it shipped."

"Okay, that takes care of clothes and Christmas. But what about day-to-day stuff—like groceries or dog food for Killer or grain for cows or horses?"

Muscles flexed and shifted beneath the white T-shirt as he shrugged dismissively. "My place is closer to two other towns than it is to Wolf Creek. I can buy all that stuff in either place."

"Hmm. It sounds as if you're avoiding Wolf Creek on purpose."

She took a drink of cold soda and waited. He didn't answer.

"A person might assume you don't like the people in Wolf Creek," she said thoughtfully.

"You think?" His voice was softly derisive.

She leaned forward, to better see his expression in the dim light. "I can understand your not wanting to see the Kerrigans, *nobody* likes dealing with Harlan and Lonnie, and you certainly might feel you have cause to dislike them. I'll even concede you probably didn't want to deal with me or Trey—I admit I wasn't too comfortable the one time I ran into you in the Saloon. I remember my mother going postal and screaming at your mother in the grocery store after Mike's funeral. You probably thought all Harpers were slightly crazy. But that's only five people out of the entire town. There are lots of other residents in Wolf Creek who are perfectly nice and don't come with baggage."

"If you say so."

"You don't agree?"

"No." He sat forward and was about to push upright when she reached out and impulsively caught his arm, stopping him.

"Surely you don't blame everyone in Wolf Creek for what happened to you when Mike died."

"You have no idea what happened to me after Mike died." His voice was grim.

"No," she said slowly. "I suppose I only know what I later learned from gossip. I was only twelve years old at the time. I know what happened at my house—my mother took to her bed after the funeral. It took her three long years to die of grief but she was determined. For my dad, losing Mike was terrible but losing Mom was more than he could take—he passed away in his sleep when I was eighteen. The doctors said he had a massive heart attack but I know mourning caused his death."

Chase covered her hand with his. His calloused palm gently pressed hers against the warm, hair-roughened strength of his forearm. The gesture was both comforting and arousing.

"I'm sorry," he said gruffly. "You were just a kid. It must have been rough."

"It was." She scanned his face, trying to read his expression. "But I'm beginning to think it was just as bad, if not worse, for you."

His features hardened. "Maybe not."

His hand left hers and he rose to look down at her. "I'd like to get an early start in the morning. Are you ready to turn in?"

Raine wanted to ask him why he wouldn't talk about those days after Mike died, but he clearly was finished with the conversation.

He walked silently beside her and waited until she was inside her room with the dead bolt firmly in place, before he left her. She drew back the drape on the front window just far enough to see him enter his own room three doors down, Killer padding at his side.

There was an aura of solitary containment about him that was striking. Raine wished he would tell her about the days and months after Mike died. While she'd been struggling to cope with her parents and their overwhelming grief, what had it been like for Chase at seventeen, locked in a prison cell? Was that where he'd gotten the scars she'd noticed on his chest and back when he'd been working at the forge on his ranch? Or had those come later, during fights with criminals while working as a bounty hunter?

She'd thought she knew who Chase McCloud was—the teenager whose reckless driving had killed her beloved brother, the man who lived a violent life chasing criminals.

Now she wasn't sure whether any of what she'd believed about him for the last fifteen years was true.

Chapter Six

Raine slipped into a cool cotton tee and pajama shorts. Far from sleepy, she took her phone card from her purse. She stacked pillows against the headboard and stretched her legs out on the muted blue-toned bedspread before dialing the Saloon's number in Wolf Creek.

"Hi, Charlotte," she said when her assistant manager answered. "How's everything going—any emergencies?"

"None so far," Charlotte responded.

"In fact, it's been so quiet I'm starting to worry. Shouldn't we have had a fight or a cranky customer or something by now? How can I flex my 'boss' muscles if nothing happens?"

Raine laughed. "Don't say that aloud or you'll jinx yourself and tomorrow will be chaos."

"Hmm. Good point. Seriously, Raine, all's quiet here. The only thing I'm concerned about is the Liquor Board inspection—the office called today and said the inspector will be here day after tomorrow. I'm guessing you'll need to be here to deal with him yourself, right?"

"Yes, I will. Damn. I expected the office to call six weeks ago—talk about bad timing." Raine sighed. "Nothing I can do about it now, I'll have to come home."

"Sorry, Raine. You know I'd be glad to deal with it if you want me to."

"Thanks, Charlotte, but I really need to talk to the inspector. You can join us, though, so if this comes up in the future, you'll be prepared."

"Sounds good. How are things going with you? Any new information about Trey?"

"Yes, thank God. Tonight we talked to a motel clerk here in Henderson who remembers seeing Trey the night he disappeared."

"That's wonderful news! What about the bar in Billings—did anyone remember seeing him there?"

"No, and my instinct tells me he wasn't there."

"Oh." Silence fell. "I'm sorry, Raine."

"Me, too. And there's bad news—a store clerk remembers seeing Trey's SUV but two men, neither of them Trey, were driving it."

"Oh, no." Charlotte gasped softly. "What does that mean?"

"Chase said I should hold on to my gut belief that Trey isn't hurt. Just because someone else may have been driving his car doesn't mean he's not okay."

"So that's not necessarily the worst of bad news. It could be those men stole

Trey's car when it was parked some-where and he was nowhere near it, right?"

"I hadn't thought of that, but you're right, of course."

"How are you coping with the bounty hunter?" Charlotte asked.

"Fine. He seems very good at his job. For the first time since Trey disappeared, I feel confident that everything possible is being done to find him."

"That's wonderful. I'm so glad." Char-lotte's sincerity carried clearly over the line. "I know how worried you've been."

"I'm still worried, but at least, I know I'm doing something proactive and not just sitting at home, hoping and praying he'll be found."

"And I'm sure you'll get results. In fact, I'm going to tell the cook to start planning a welcome-home party for Trey. What's it like spending all day and night with the mysterious, gorgeous Mr. McCloud?" Charlotte teased, lightening the mood.

The question startled Raine and immediately, a series of vignettes flashed through her mind—Chase washed in moonlight by the motel pool; Chase solemnly shaking the storekeeper's hand; Chase pulling her close as they crossed the room to the booth in the Bull 'n' Bash, then nuzzling her neck when they sat.

What's it like to spend time with Chase? He's difficult, charming, sexy and too intriguing, she thought. None of which she'd admit to Charlotte.

"I'm learning a lot about investigative procedures," she answered. "In fact, if Trey ever disappears again, I might not need to hire someone to find him. I can do it myself."

Charlotte laughed. "So what's next— where do you go from here?"

Raine spent the next ten minutes filling Charlotte in on her plans for the next day and listening to Charlotte's droll recital of the latest battle in the ongoing war between the restaurant's grouchy dishwasher and temperamental cook. She rang off after promising to return to Wolf Creek for the upcoming inspection.

Relieved to learn all was well at both the restaurant and Saloon, she switched off the bedside lamp and went to sleep.

At ten o'clock the following morning, they left Killer in the SUV with the windows lowered to let a breeze cool the interior and entered a truck stop just south of Henderson. The state trooper Chase had arranged to meet in the café was sitting at a booth near the back.

"Trooper Smith?" Chase asked.

"Yes—are you McCloud?" The uniformed officer started to stand but Chase waved him back.

"Don't get up. We'll join you, if you don't mind."

"Of course not."

Raine slid across the booth's bench seat and Chase joined her.

"Dispatch passed on your message— said you're looking for a man who may have been at the scene of an accident a few weeks ago?"

"That's right." Chase took Trey's photo from his shirt pocket and slid it across the table. "We've confirmed his vehicle was stopped near Henderson when a semi overturned a couple of weeks ago."

"I remember the truck—made a helluva mess on the road. Took us a couple of hours to clear the scene. But I don't remember another vehicle being involved."

"His SUV was in the traffic halted by the truck accident. We don't have any reason to believe he was actually involved in the wreck."

"Ah." The trooper nodded and picked up the photo, tilting it to study it more closely. Then he slowly shook his head. "I'm sorry, I don't remember seeing him."

Raine's hope that their luck gaining information from the motel clerk would continue when they talked to the trooper evaporated.

Chase asked several more questions

about the highway accident before they left the trooper finishing his morning coffee and doughnut break in the café.

"I was hoping he'd give us a lead," Raine said as they fastened seat belts.

"It was a long shot. Unlikely the trooper on the scene of an accident would remember a driver not involved, especially since Trey apparently didn't approach him."

"I suppose so." Raine was frustrated. "I have to go back to Wolf Creek," she said suddenly.

Chase's hand stilled on the ignition key and he turned his head to look at her. "Burned out on man-hunting already?"

She returned his cool gaze with a level stare. "No, definitely not. But I have a business appointment at the Saloon tomorrow and I'm the only person who can take care of it."

"Then we'll go home." He switched on the ignition and backed out of the parking slot.

"Not until tonight," she said stubbornly. "I don't have to be at the Saloon until late tomorrow morning."

"Whatever you say. What's the next stop on the map?"

She retrieved the folded map and scanned the road ahead. "A gas station just off the highway, about twenty-five miles."

Chase didn't reply. The SUV picked up speed as they headed south once again.

"It's not as if I want to go home," she murmured, almost to herself.

Chase glanced at her and shrugged. "Few people can put their full-time jobs on hold to spend time investigating a missing person."

"Which is one of the reasons your company does well, I suppose?"

He laughed, a deep amused chuckle that sent shivers over Raine. "Oh, yeah," he drawled. "That and the fact we're very good at what we do."

"Yes, you are," she conceded. "Sorry. I'm just frustrated and annoyed that I have to go home and can't continue with the search. What will you do next?"

"I'll drop you off in Wolf Creek and stop at my place for clean clothes, probably check in with my brother, Luke, and my folks. Then I'll head south again and continue questioning potential witnesses."

"There's something else I need to ask you about."

"What's that?"

"I received an invitation to Zach and Jessie's wedding." Raine glanced sideways at Chase, trying to gauge his reaction. "I'd like to go but I'm not sure I should, especially since it's being held in your mother's garden. Do you think your family would mind if I was there?"

"If it doesn't bother you, I'm sure it's fine with them."

"Are you being polite or do you really think your parents will be okay with this?" she demanded, not sure she should believe him.

"You actually think I'd bother lying to you to be polite?" His voice sounded amused and a little surprised.

"People have been known to tell little white lies to avoid upsetting other people," she said. "Although come to think of it, I'm guessing you probably don't bother with polite lies to ease social situations."

"If I have, I don't remember it," he said. "But if you're worried, I'll ask my parents."

"Good," Raine said with relief. "Wait… if they said they weren't okay with my being there, would you tell me? You wouldn't try to save my feelings, would you? Because it would be worse if I went and *then* found out they really didn't want me at their daughter's wedding."

Chase shook his head, lifting an eyebrow in disbelief. "Didn't we just have this conversation? I wouldn't lie to you. Besides, this is Jessie's wedding. Trust me, I know my sister. If it wasn't okay with her for you to be a guest, you would never have gotten an invitation."

"Oh." Raine mulled this over. She wasn't totally convinced, but decided there really wasn't anything further she could do. "Okay, then. Good. That's good to know."

"I didn't realize you knew Zach well," Chase said.

"We were friends in high school. We didn't keep in touch after graduation, but he's stopped in the Saloon several times since he came home to help his mother run the ranch." She paused, shaking her head. "I can't believe your family didn't guess Rowdy was his son. Zach brought him into the restaurant for lunch a few weeks ago and I swear, that boy looks just like him."

"It never occurred to any of us that Jessie would fall in love with a Kerrigan. Much less have a child with him and then keep it a secret from all of us, including Zach, for nearly four years."

"You don't hold it against Zach that Harlan is his uncle, do you? Or that Lonnie is his cousin? He's nothing like them..."

"No, he's not," Chase interrupted her. "If he were, there's no way he'd be marrying my little sister." He shook his head in disbelief. "She told me that's why she didn't tell us—because she was afraid no McCloud would ever accept a marriage between one of us and a Kerrigan."

"But Luke married Zach's sister—didn't that make Jessie reconsider?"

"Jessie said their marriage happened four years after she made the decision not to tell us Zach was Rowdy's father. She thought it was too late to change her story."

"And then Zach came home..." Raine said.

"Yeah. And unlike the rest of us, he took one look at Rowdy and knew he was the father."

"I'm glad he and Jessie worked out their differences, for everyone's sake, but especially for Rowdy."

They spent the rest of the day methodically checking out places along the highway where Trey might have stopped but came up empty. Raine tried to remain optimistic but was discouraged that she had to return home before they learned something definitive.

It was nearly ten-thirty that night when Chase turned into Raine's driveway in Wolf Creek.

"I'll get your bag out of the back."

"Thanks." Raine took her purse and got out. Killer squeezed between the two front seats and bounded after her. Startled, she laughed and patted the soft black fur between his ears. He trotted beside her up the sidewalk and across the porch, waiting while she unlocked the door before nudging it farther open with his nose.

"Killer, stop that. Behave yourself." Chase joined them, leaning around Raine to drop her bag inside and drag the inquisitive big dog away from the door. "You don't have a light out here?" he asked, frowning as he scanned the dark porch, lit only by moon glow.

"Yes, but I didn't turn it on when I left."

"I'll get an automatic timer for you. Motion sensor lamps are a good idea, too. You need better security."

She laughed softly. "This is Wolf Creek, Chase, not Seattle. Very little crime ever happens here. I feel perfectly safe."

"Humor me. Extra security can't hurt."

"All right." She felt warmed and somehow cherished by his concern.

Killer nudged her knee with his nose and she bent to give him a quick hug. "So long, Killer. Behave yourself." Upright once more, she patted his nose affectionately.

"Yeah, like that's gonna happen," Chase said wryly. "Go get in the car, Killer."

The Rottweiler woofed softly, bumping Raine's leg with his shoulder as he bounded across the porch toward the sidewalk. He knocked Raine off balance. She stumbled backward against Chase and instantly, his arms wrapped around her, holding her safe. Raine caught her breath. His body was a solid, warm wall at her back, his right hand splayed over her midriff, his thumb against the lower curve of her breast. For one brief moment, neither of them moved. Then Chase bent his head, his lips brushing against her ear.

"Are you all right?" His voice was a low, raspy rumble.

She felt it vibrate through her body all the way to her toes.

"Yes, I—" she drew in a shaky breath "—I'm fine."

He released her slowly, his hands lingering as if reluctant to leave the curve of her waist.

"I'll be leaving town before noon tomorrow."

She turned, looking up at him. The moonlight barely penetrated the deep overhang of the porch and shadowed his face, only heightening his mysteriousness. "You'll call if you find out anything new about Trey?"

He nodded. "I'm guessing I can reach you at the restaurant or Saloon most of the time and not here at the house?"

"Yes," she murmured.

He cupped her face in his hand, his fingers calloused and faintly abrasive against her skin. She waited breathlessly, hoping and fearing he would kiss her.

He smoothed the pad of his thumb across her lower lip in a slow, heart-stopping caress and then released her.

"Take care."

He took the steps in easy strides. Raine leaned against the doorjamb, grateful for its support since her legs felt too unsteady to hold her upright. He backed out of her driveway, flicking the headlights at her twice, and she waved goodbye, then went inside.

She showered and went through her usual routine to get ready for bed in a daze, her mind whirling. She'd dated her share of men over the years but Chase wasn't like any other. Not only did they have a history together, but he affected her as no one else ever had.

She'd been focusing on business and putting her personal life second for as long as she could remember, certainly since her father died and she'd taken over running the family business with Trey when she was eighteen. Determined to salvage some sort of security and success from the shambles of her family life, she'd never once allowed a man to become important to her.

Even now, she didn't think she'd *allowed* Chase to be important to her—he simply was. It felt as if she'd been waiting for him, marking time with the occasional casual boyfriend until he returned.

Stricken, she stared at her reflection in the mirror, her hand wielding the hairbrush frozen in midair.

What am I? Sleeping Beauty waiting for the Prince to return and kiss me awake?

It wasn't like she was in love with him. Was she?

I can't be, she told herself. *Falling in love at first sight only happens in fairy tales. Lust, sure. She'd admit to lust. Who wouldn't? The man was tall, dark, magnetic. Not to mention sexy as sin.*

She finished brushing her hair and

went to bed, determined not to think about Chase. But her dreams were filled with him, the imaginary kisses they shared growing hotter with each succeeding fantasy.

Raine spent the following morning in her office, a medium-size room tucked between the restaurant and the Saloon, dealing with a small mountain of paperwork. Charlotte was efficient and organized but there were some decisions that could only be made by Raine and those had stacked up during her absence.

She was flipping through supply order sheets, trying to make sense of a distributor invoice for delivery of an order she was sure had neither been placed nor received, when someone knocked on the door.

"Come in," she called distractedly, still concentrating on the stack of order forms.

"Good morning, Raine."

Harlan Kerrigan crossed the threshold, closing the door behind him.

"Mr. Kerrigan." She pressed the call

button hidden beneath the desk's center drawer, then stood. "What can I do for you?"

"I wanted to discuss a matter with you, if you have a moment."

Raine pointedly looked at her watch. "Of course, but only a moment, I'm afraid. I've been out of town for a few days and have a mountain of paperwork to get through today." She gestured at the wooden chair facing her desk. "Please, have a seat."

Just as he settled into the chair and Raine sat down, Charlotte entered, looking inquiringly at Raine, then her gaze flicked to Harlan. She lifted an eyebrow in obvious surprise and speculation.

"Charlotte, would you bring two coffees? I'm taking a ten-minute break to discuss something with Mr. Kerrigan before tackling the distributor invoice situation."

"Of course." Charlotte grinned, pointedly leaving the door ajar as she disappeared down the hall.

"Now, is it time for the Chamber of Commerce's annual fund-raiser? As always, I'll be happy to donate toward the cost of the Chamber's booth at the county fair." Raine didn't miss Harlan's annoyed expression and knew he wasn't pleased she'd limited their time to ten minutes.

He propped his ankle on the opposite knee and removed his Stetson. Gone was the visible annoyance, his face smoothed into affable lines.

He was impeccably dressed and Raine realized she'd never seen Harlan anything less than meticulous. The light-weight gray summer suit he wore had a knife-edge crease in the slacks; his black cowboy boots gleamed with polish. The white Stetson he'd settled on his knee was spotless, as was the white shirt he wore with his suit. The bolo tie at his collar had a gold nugget that matched the hammered gold ring on his right hand.

He was the perfect picture of a suc-

cessful, responsible Western business-
man yet Raine didn't trust him an inch.
She'd rarely had dealings with him in the
years since she and Trey had taken over
the Harper-owned businesses. Local
gossip said Harlan's time was increasingly centered in the state capital. She
wouldn't be surprised to hear he had political aspirations.

"I'm sure the Chamber will be pleased
to receive your contribution—I'll be glad
to deliver your check. However, I wanted
to talk to you about another matter. I've
heard a rumor that I find difficult to
believe, Raine, and I felt compelled to
share my concerns with you."

"Really? What rumor is that?" Raine
wasn't buying his avuncular concern.
She was sure an agenda of his own had
brought him to her door and she wished
he'd get on with telling her so she could
get back to her waiting invoices.

"Here we go." Charlotte breezed into
the room, carrying a tray and forestalling
Harlan's response. "Two coffees. Both

black?" She looked at Harlan and received an annoyed nod.

"Thanks, Charlotte. Will you tell Kenny I'll be ready to go over the invoices with him in about ten minutes?"

"Sure, boss." Charlotte winked at Raine and left the room, purposely leaving the door ajar once again.

"I'm sorry, Harlan, but it's chaos around here today. You were saying?" Raine prompted.

"I can see you're busy so I'll keep this brief. I've heard a rumor that you've hired Chase McCloud to look for your brother."

"That's true."

"I'm sure if your parents were here, they'd urge you to rethink this decision. In their absence, I must urge you to reconsider, as well."

He leaned forward in his chair, his gaze shrewd and hard, probing hers.

Raine lifted her coffee cup and sipped, taking her time. "I appreciate your concern, Harlan, but I fail to see why

you're so worried. I've hired a professional to search for my missing brother.
Frankly, I feel fortunate that a man as ex-
perienced as Chase is available and
willing to take on Trey's case."

"Fortunate? Surely you realize
McCloud is an ex-convict? You were only
a child when he was locked away so
perhaps you don't know the full story and
don't realize just how dangerous this man
is."

"I was twelve when my brother Mike
died," Raine said. "And although I
don't know all the details of the case, I
don't see how a fifteen-year-old car
accident is material to my situation at
this point."

"The man was held responsible for the
death of your brother."

"I understand the jury found Chase
guilty," Raine agreed.

"You know he may have a hidden
agenda in taking on this search for your
brother?"

"A hidden agenda? Like what?"

"Like revenge against your family. After all, the death of a Harper sent him to jail."

Anger flared, bright and hot, and Raine carefully set down her coffee cup on the polished desk surface. "My brother died, Harlan, but it was testimony from you and Lonnie that sent Chase to jail. If he wants revenge against anyone, I'm guessing it's far more likely to involve you or Lonnie. Perhaps you should be more concerned about your own situation, and less about mine."

"Is that what he told you?"

"Chase hasn't said anything to me about you," she lied. "But any rational-thinking person could look at the basic facts of the case and conclude Chase might feel he has cause to dislike you and Lonnie."

"I'm afraid we'll have to agree to disagree," he said after a tension-charged moment. He glanced around the office. "I see you haven't changed much in here since you took over."

"Not a lot," Raine agreed, wondering

where he was going now with the conversation.

"Your father and I didn't often see eye-to-eye on issues, either. If he'd listened to me, you would have inherited businesses with a much higher net worth." He stared at her, his eyes cold. "You might consider that when you think about your association with the McClouds."

"Are you threatening me, Harlan?" Raine asked softly, holding on to her temper by a thread.

She expected him to deny her charge, but his next comment came out of left field.

"Do you have any leads in the search for your brother?" he asked abruptly.

She wasn't sure why, but she instinctively didn't want to reveal the truth. "No."

"The police haven't found anything?"

"No. It's as if Trey dropped off the face of the earth."

"I'm sorry to hear that." Harlan shook his head, his expression properly sympathetic, but Raine thought she detected a flash of satisfaction. He stood, set his untouched coffee cup on the desk, and settled his hat on his head. "If there's anything I can do to aid in finding Trey, don't hesitate to come to me."

Raine rose to face him across the desk. "Thanks for your offer, although I can't think of anything at the moment."

"Nevertheless, the offer is open, should something arise. I'll let you get back to your work." He nodded, touched the brim of his hat and left the room.

Raine dropped into her chair. What was Harlan up to? She didn't believe for a moment that he was genuinely concerned about her, nor about Trey. What was the real reason he'd questioned her about Chase?

At roughly the same time Harlan was leaving Raine's office, Chase was driving south to resume the search where he and Raine had left off the day before. He turned up the volume on the radio but the SUV still felt oddly quiet without her.

Furthermore, the interior of the SUV held the scent of her perfume. When Killer leaned forward from the backseat and rested his chin on Chase's shoulder, he realized the Rottweiler smelled faintly of Raine, too.

"Damn, dog," he· said, exasperated. "Did she spray you with the stuff?"

Killer gave him a reproachful look and retreated, stretching out on the seat with his head on his paws.

Chase eyed him in the rearview mirror and sighed.

"All right, I'm sorry. I know she hugged you at least a dozen times and that's probably why you smell like her perfume."

Killer glanced up at him with dignified reproof before shutting his eyes.

"Great," Chase muttered. "Now my dog's ignoring me."

He stopped for gas in midafternoon and on impulse, bought a car deodorizer at the checkout stand. He hung the four-inch tree-shaped felt on his rearview mirror but within an hour he ripped it off and threw it out the window. The pine scent gave him a headache but at least the lingering trace of Raine's perfume in the SUV's interior was gone. Unfortunately, the next morning when he climbed behind the wheel, he could smell her perfume again.

There was no escaping it. She was imprinted on his brain.

It was annoying as hell.

Four days went by and Raine still hadn't heard from Chase. She had left daily messages on his answering machine but he hadn't returned her calls. He'd told her he'd phone if he learned anything new so she assumed he had nothing to report. Nevertheless, his silence was unnerving.

Where was he? Why didn't he call? At the very least, he could tell her how many towns and truck stops he'd eliminated from his search list.

She spent her days from midmorning

until after ten at night at work, staying busy with the many details necessary to keep both the Saloon, restaurant and motel running smoothly. Without Trey to share the workload, there were more than enough tasks to fill her hours.

On Friday night, she left the office just after ten-thirty, spoke briefly with the bartender on duty in the Saloon and exchanged hellos with several regular customers. Then she left, the muted sounds of laughter and music from the Saloon following her across the street to her car.

A month ago, she would have said goodnight to Trey before leaving for home and they would have taken a few moments to exchange highlights of their workdays.

Where are you Trey? she thought, for what surely must have been the thousandth time since he'd disappeared.

"And damn it, Chase, why haven't you called?" she murmured in frustration as she climbed the shallow steps to her porch, keys in hand.

"Because I didn't want to talk to you."

The deep male voice growled from the shadows on her left.

"Chase?" Her voice shook with fear and adrenaline.

"Yeah."

A dark form rose from one of the wicker chairs in the far corner and came toward her.

"You startled me." She lowered her hands, pressing her right palm just over her pounding heart. "Why didn't you want to talk to me?"

"Because I didn't have anything new to tell you…"

He kept walking and Raine took a step back, unnerved.

"…and because you're driving me crazy."

"What?" she got out, retreating another step as he loomed over her. There was something faintly threatening about him, an aura of danger that made her heart beat faster.

He bent nearer, his lips brushing her temple as he drew in a deep breath before he spoke. "I can't get the smell of your perfume out of my car."

"I..."

"I miss arguing with you." He lifted a hand and tucked a strand of hair behind her ear, lingering to trace the curve of her earlobe. "And Killer's been moping ever since we dropped you off."

"I'm sorry, I don't—" She was bewildered and dazed by the possibility he had missed her as much as she had missed him.

"And the worst part," he interrupted her, "is that I don't like your being too far away to touch." He slipped his arms around her waist and tugged her closer until her body rested against his from chest to thigh. "Or kiss."

He bent his head and brushed soft kisses against the corners of her lips before cupping her face, tilting her chin up to take her mouth with his. Raine threaded her fingers through the thick silk of his hair and held him closer, feeding the heat that roared between them with the pressure of his mouth against hers, the stroke of his tongue as he licked her bottom lip. She groaned, lifting to better fit her body into the hard angles of his. His arms tightened and he cupped her bottom, lifting her to fit the soft cove of her hips against his hard arousal.

"God, you taste good," he muttered, nuzzling the sensitive skin of her neck. Her head dropped back against his shoulder, her eyes drifting closed.

"Should we be doing this?" she murmured in a last bid for sanity.

"Oh, yeah." His voice was thick. "We should have done it days ago." His lips reached the sensitive spot where shoulder met throat and Raine's toes curled, desire heating her skin, unfurling tendrils of aching need. She could barely think.

"Um…But it's never wise to mix business with…this…and I'm your client." Was that really important? She wondered hazily. She wasn't sure anymore.

"So fire me." He nudged her back against the door frame, pinned her there with his body and covered her mouth with his.

Heat exploded in her midsection and spread like wildfire. His tongue stroked against hers in blatant invitation and her nipples tightened painfully.

When he finally lifted his head, she felt thoroughly ravished. Her blouse was tugged out of her waistband, his hand warm against the sensitive skin of her midriff.

"Let's go inside," he muttered, his lips barely moving against the curve of her ear.

"I don't think that's a good idea," she said shakily, shivering when his hand left her midriff for the small of her back. He urged her upward and her heels left the floor, her body seeking a more intimate fit against his.

"You're kidding, right?" he growled, nudging his hips against hers.

"I wish I wasn't." Regret filled her voice. "I need to think about this, Chase."

He sighed, lifting his head just far enough to search her face. "You're sure about that?"

"Yes," she lied.

"All right. But we're both going to be sorry."

"You think?" She managed a smile, knowing refusing him would probably keep her awake for hours.

"Oh, yeah. I hate cold showers. Sure you won't change your mind and ask me in?"

"No," she murmured, fighting the urge to say yes.

"Damn," he said, his voice husky. "Then I guess I'll have to let you go in alone." His mouth covered hers again. Long moments later, he unwound her arms from around his neck and stepped back, bending his head to press one last kiss against her lips. "Next time, say yes." He turned and left her.

Chapter Seven

Despite dreaming about making love to Raine for most of the night, Chase woke early the next morning. A midmorning phone call to his mother gained him an invitation to lunch and just before noon, he drove down the long ranch road and parked in front of his parents' house. Killer jumped out beside him, his deep bark greeting the black-and-tan dog standing on the porch. His mother appeared, smiling with delight.

"I thought it might be you when I heard Muttly barking," she called.

Chase opened the gate and Killer bounded inside to race up the sidewalk and exchange hellos with the older dog on the porch.

"I think he missed you," he teased as Killer nudged Margaret and she bent to pet him.

"We missed him, too," she replied. "And you. Come into the kitchen. Your dad and I are getting food ready for the grill."

Chase wrapped an arm around her shoulders and dropped a kiss on the top of her head. "Dad's barbecuing steaks for lunch?"

"Yes, and you can light the grill in about fifteen minutes."

"Great." He followed her down the hallway to the kitchen. "Hey, Dad."

John McCloud looked up from the marble cutting board where he was trimming fat from thick New York steaks with a wicked-looking knife. "Glad you could make it, Chase.

There's cold beer or lemonade in the fridge."

Chase opted for icy lemonade.

Margaret handed him a bag of corn on the cob and a brown paper bag. "Will you shuck the corn for me?"

"Sure." He sat at the table, the open bag at his feet, and began to strip away green leaves and pale corn silk. "How have you two been? Anything new?"

"Not with us," Margaret said pointedly. "We're fine. You're the one with stories to tell, aren't you?"

He glanced up. His dad had paused, knife in hand, to look at him and his mother's bright eyes were curious.

"I'm guessing it's safe to assume you've heard about the case I'm working on," he said.

It wasn't really a question and Chase didn't need their nods of agreement, but he waited for them, nonetheless, before he continued. "Trey Harper disappeared almost three weeks ago and his sister hired me to look for him. Not a lot more to tell you. We found a motel clerk in Henderson who talked to him on the night he disappeared. And a store clerk remembers seeing his car being driven by two unknown men. Other than that, nothing."

"We heard Trey Harper was missing, of course. It was all folks talked about for the first week or so. It's still a topic that comes up every time I go into town—a terrible thing. The sheriff's office hasn't had any luck, either?" John asked.

"No. Their investigation turned up zero information. A store clerk confirmed he sold gas to two men driving a silver SUV with Trey's vanity plates. But except for that one sighting, the vehicle has disappeared, too, despite a statewide alert. No one's tried to access Harper's bank account or use his credit cards, either."

Margaret's expression was troubled. "It doesn't sound good, does it."

Chase shook his head. "If it weren't for

Raine, I'd be convinced I'm looking for a dead body. But she insists her brother's alive."

"What makes her think he's alive if you're convinced he's probably dead?" John asked, surprised.

"Trey's her twin. According to Raine, they've always had some kind of bond. She swears she feels it when something bad happens to her brother and she'd know if he were dead."

"Really?" Margaret's eyebrows raised, her expression thoughtful. "I've read about twins having psychic connections but never personally known anyone who claimed it was true."

"I don't know if it's true or not. All I have is Raine's word."

"I was surprised to hear you signed on to look for her brother," John said.

"You mean because he's a Harper?" Chase asked bluntly.

"Yeah."

"It's business."

His dad looked unconvinced but his

mother considered him for a moment and then nodded with decision.

"Well, I'm glad you're trying to help find him. That poor girl only has one member of her family left and it would be a shame if he disappeared and she never saw him again." She nodded emphatically, closing the subject. "We're picking up your dad's new tuxedo tomorrow—would you like us to collect yours, too?"

"Sure." Chase grinned when his dad groaned. "I hope Jessie appreciates the sacrifice we made when we agreed to wear bow ties and shirt studs for this wedding."

"I'm sure she does," Margaret said. "Although I can't for the life of me understand why men always moan about getting dressed up. Every time your father and I attend a black-tie event at the governor's mansion, he complains."

"I'm more comfortable in boots and jeans," John protested. "This is Jessie's wedding, so I suppose it's worth a little discomfort if it makes her happy."

"Yeah," Chase said. "Is everything ready for the big night—anything I can do for you or Jessie?"

"Not that I can think of," Margaret said. "Your dad and Luke finished setting up the small platform on the lawn for the altar…the caterer is the same one I always use and I know she's absolutely reliable…the photographer is dependable…I think everything's set. I'm glad Jessie decided to have the wedding in our garden—makes it so much easier, especially since the flowers are at their best this month. Just make sure you're here," Margaret warned. "Don't call me from some foreign country and cancel because of a work emergency, okay?"

"I won't," Chase promised. "That reminds me—Raine told me she'd like to come but she's worried you and Dad might not want her at the house."

"Why the hell wouldn't we?" John asked, clearly taken aback.

"I think she's convinced the family

somehow blames her and Trey for her mother's actions after Mike died."

"That's crazy," John said bluntly.

"Of course we don't!" Margaret said immediately. "Why would we? She was a little girl when it happened—how could she be held responsible for how her mother reacted? In fact," Margaret said, shaking her head, "I've never really harbored any bad feelings toward Anna Harper for what she said to me back then. She was beside herself with grief."

"I told Raine you wouldn't blame her," Chase said. "But she insisted she didn't want to ruin Jessie's wedding day so I said I'd run her worries by you."

"Tell her she's more than welcome." Margaret took the bowl of shucked corn from Chase and handed him a box of matches. "Why don't you go light the grill while we finish up in here."

Chase walked out onto the patio, mulling over the conversation. He hadn't been sure how his parents would feel about his working with Raine, but apparently, his mother had just given him her seal of approval.

Women, he thought. *I'll never understand them, not even my mother.*

"Dad said I'd find you out here."

Chase looked over his shoulder. Luke walked toward him across the sunny patio, carrying two frosty bottles of beer.

"Thanks." Chase took one of the bottles from Luke's outstretched hand and tipped it, swallowing the cold liquid with appreciation. He wiped the back of his forearm across his brow and gazed at his brother. "What are you doing here in the middle of the day?"

"Rachel talked to Mom this morning and she mentioned you were expected here for lunch. I thought I'd come by and find out what's new."

"Yeah, right. Why are you really here?"

"I heard Trey Harper's sister hired you to look for him."

"You heard right."

"And she's traveling with you?"

"Yeah."

"I thought you always worked alone."

"I do. This is an exception."

Luke lifted an eyebrow in disbelief. "You made an exception to a hard-and-fast rule—for a Harper? Why am I having a hard time understanding this?"

"Maybe because I'm having a hard time myself," Chase growled.

"So why did you take the case? And why did you let her go with you?"

"She says her brother received a letter from an anonymous writer telling him to be at the Bull 'n' Bash in Billings if he wanted to learn what really happened fifteen years ago when Mike died."

Lucas's gaze sharpened. "Who sent the letter?"

"She doesn't know. I want to find Trey and the letter so I can track it to its source. Whatever the writer knows, I want to know."

"Do you think it was one of the Kerrigans?"

"Hard to believe either Harlan or

Lonnie would grow a conscience after all these years. No—" Chase shook his head "—there must have been someone else who found out what happened that night. Maybe they were there. Maybe Lonnie got drunk and told somebody. I don't know, but I plan to find out."

"How's the search for Trey Harper going?"

"It's not. Nothing but dead ends after one solid sighting in Henderson."

"Damn," Lucas said with feeling.

"Yeah. But it's early. I'll find him. And when I do, I want a look at that letter."

Raine turned off the highway, following several other vehicles down the graveled road leading to John and Margaret McCloud's home. She found a space in the crowded parking area and eased her car into the narrow slot. The early-evening sunshine had lost the searing heat of afternoon but it was still very warm. She draped her silk evening shawl over her arm. It was a shade darker than the pale green, off-the-shoulder sundress she wore with a simple gold locket and gold filigree earrings. The delicate metal lace earrings were four inches long and glittered against her hair, hanging loose to brush her shoulders. Her careful inspection in the mirror before leaving home earlier had convinced Raine that she didn't look nervous, despite the flutter of butterflies in her stomach, and that she'd reached her goal of understated elegance. The last thing she wanted to do was stand out from the crowd. In fact, she hoped to remain unseen by the McCloud family throughout the wedding ceremony, join the receiving line to congratulate Zach and his bride and then slip away unnoticed before the reception began.

Despite Chase's assurances to the contrary, she couldn't imagine his father, mother, sister or brother were looking forward to seeing a Harper at a McCloud family wedding. She was convinced her presence would be uncomfortable for them on a day that should be filled with only happiness.

On the other hand, she and Zach had been friends since high school and she wanted to be there to wish him well when he married the woman he clearly adored.

She hoped she'd be able to satisfy both her wishes—share Zach's joy on his wedding day and avoid any potentially painful confrontations with the bride's family.

Smoothing her skirt one last time, Raine lifted her chin, squared her shoulders and walked carefully over the graveled ranch yard, mindful of the delicate leather of her heels.

Several couples were a few steps ahead of her when she reached the open gate, intricately crafted to match the wrought iron fence. Raine trailed her fingertips over a smooth black iron curve, convinced Chase had likely hammered and shaped it in his forge. She followed the chattering group of guests as they strolled along a flagstone pathway edged by lush flower beds and reached the backyard. The beautiful lawn and garden had been meticulously groomed and decorated for the ceremony and reception.

Dozens of wedding guests filled all but a few of the white-painted wooden folding chairs arranged in rows on the plush grass. The chairs faced away from the house and toward a raised altar at the far edge of the lawn. Sprays of pink, white and red roses twined and draped the arching trellis creating a fragrant bower over the altar. A white cloth covered the center aisle between the rows of seats and the end chair in every second row had a satin bow and bouquet of roses clipped to its edge.

A quartet of strings and woodwinds occupied a corner of the flagstone patio, the Debussy melody they were playing underscoring the murmurs and muted laughter from the seated guests.

"Are you a guest of the bride or the groom?"

Raine started glancing around to see a fresh-faced young man in a tuxedo, looking at her expectantly.

"The groom," she said. "And I'd like to sit near the back, please."

"Sure." He stuck out his arm with self-conscious chivalry.

"I'll seat the lady, David."

Raine turned, her eyes widening. She'd thought Chase was handsome in faded jeans and dusty cowboy boots, but in a tuxedo, he could stop traffic. "Hello," she managed to say.

"Hello." His gaze swept her from head to toe, then returned with disconcerting slowness until he looked into her eyes again. The heat in his left no doubt that he liked what he saw.

Raine felt his slow survey as if he'd stroked his hand over her bare skin. Her body responded with heat that began low in her belly, spreading swiftly until she burned all over.

He stepped closer, took her hand in his and tucked it into the crook of his elbow.

He bent his head, his lips brushing her ear, making her shiver, as he spoke. "I'm supposed to sit up front with the rest of the family."

Raine glanced at the first two rows of chairs, filling with McCloud and Kerrigan relatives.

"Go ahead, I'll sit back here," she whispered, determined to remain unnoticed.

He studied her face for a moment, then shrugged. "Whatever you say."

He drew her with him to two empty seats on the aisle, three rows from the back. He stood back to let her enter, then sat beside her just as the pastor climbed the two steps to the altar and faced the guests. Zach and a man Raine didn't recognize followed the pastor across the lawn and took their places at the foot of the steps. The three men faced the audience and stood with their hands clasped in front of them, looking down the cloth-covered aisle.

"Don't you have to join your family?"

Raine whispered, leaning into Chase to keep from being overheard. His shoulder pressed against hers, the unique scent of soap and hint of after-shave she'd come to associate with only him reaching her nostrils.

"Not if you don't want to."

"Chase, please don't give your parents another reason to dislike me," she said softly. The older lady in the chair in front of Raine looked over her shoulder, her slight frown clearing when she recognized Raine.

"Good evening, Raine. Lovely to see you."

"Lovely to see you, too, Mrs. Plunkett."

The older woman smiled, nodded at Chase and faced forward once more.

Raine closed her eyes and sighed. "Great," she whispered to Chase. "She'll tell your mother for sure."

"Tell my mother what?" Chase lifted a questioning eyebrow.

"That you're associating with the enemy, of course."

"What makes you think my mother believes you're the enemy?" he murmured.

"Oh, do be serious, Chase," Raine whispered. "My mother yelled at your mother and threw a hysterical fit in the grocery store. Dad said Mom refused to let Margaret leave. He was afraid Mom was going to attack her."

"Honey." Chase leaned close, his voice audible only to Raine. "Mom told Dad if she'd lost a son as your mother had, she didn't think she'd have kept her sanity. I doubt my mother ever thought of anyone in your family as 'the enemy.'"

"But…" Raine began, unconvinced.

The swelling strains of "The Wedding March" interrupted her. All around them the guests rose to their feet accompanied by the rustle of clothing and murmurs of anticipation.

Raine and Chase stood, too, half turning to look toward the patio just as the wedding party left the house. Three young women in vibrant, deep rose-pink gowns were accompanied by men in tuxedos. They were followed by a little girl tossing rose petals from a beribboned basket; walking beside her was Rowdy, Jessie and Zach's son. The little boy's grave expression broke into a broad grin when he saw Chase. The grin widened when Chase winked at him; he waved exuberantly in response before the two children moved past and down the aisle.

Then John McCloud stepped through the open French doors and out onto the patio, his daughter on his arm. Jessie seemed to float toward them in a froth of white skirts, her long veil a gossamer web of pale lace over her auburn hair.

Tears misted Raine's eyes. Jessie's face was radiant as she glided down the aisle toward the altar where Zach waited.

Raine sniffed quietly, bending her head to rummage in her purse for a tissue. Without comment, Chase held out a snowy-white handkerchief and she murmured her thanks, taking it to blot her cheeks and the tears still dampening her lashes.

The ceremony was very traditional until Zach kissed his bride. Then tradition was abandoned. He turned to Rowdy, sitting with Zach's mother in the first row, and held out his arms.

Rowdy crowed with glee and raced to the altar, launching himself into his father's arms. Zach caught him and Rowdy flung one small arm around Zach's neck before he leaned over and hugged Jessie.

The guests burst out laughing, cheering as Zach took Jessie's hand, perched Rowdy on his hip, and all three left the altar for the patio. A buffet was set up along one side and round tables filled the flagstone area while others were scattered over the lawn and beneath the trees.

Chase bent to whisper in Raine's ear. "Do you always cry at weddings?"

"Yes, I'm afraid so."

"They make you sad?"

"No, they make me happy."

Chase shook his head in disbelief. "I'll never understand women."

"Excuse me?" The young usher who'd greeted Raine earlier stood in the aisle. "Your mother wanted me to tell you the photographer needs all the family gathered together, Chase."

"Tell her I'll be right there." Chase looked down at Raine. "I have to do this."

"I know, go." She gave his arm a gentle push. "Wedding photos are important to the bride and groom."

"Don't go too far. I'll be back as soon as I can."

Raine smiled noncommittally and waved him away. With luck, she thought, she'd catch Zach for a moment to wish him well and then leave before Chase finished with the photographer.

The wedding was beautiful and she was glad she came, but it was definitely time to go. She didn't belong here. She glanced around. Virginia McGonagle, whose husband owned McGonagle's Feed Store in Wolf Creek, whispered fervently to Mrs. Plunkett, both looking at her with interest. Virginia returned

Raine's nod of hello with a faintly guilty smile.

Probably feeling guilty because she's gossiping about Chase and me sitting together. Raine knew the gathering of neighbors familiar with old history between the McCloud and Harper families would soon be buzzing.

Gossip—how she hated it. She'd spent her teen and adult life ignoring rumors, however, and saw no reason to change tactics now.

All about her, the guests were standing, streaming toward the patio. Raine rose and joined the other guests. She knew nearly all of them, some as nodding acquaintances and some more personally. Wolf Creek was a small ranching community; Raine knew most of the people present probably were connected in one way or another.

The sun dropped below the horizon and long shadows stretched across the lawn. The trees were draped with strings of tiny white lights that gleamed brighter as dusk deepened and the Japanese lanterns hanging from lower limbs glowed with a rainbow of colors.

Raine accepted a glass of champagne from a young waiter and searched the crowd, relieved when she found Charlotte waving wildly from beneath a tall tree across the lawn. She inched her way through the guests to join her friend, who stood with her husband, Dan.

"We looked for you when we arrived but couldn't find you. Where were you sitting?" Charlotte demanded as Raine reached them.

"Near the back—I was late and didn't get here until just before the ceremony. What a crush." Raine gestured at the packed lawn and patio. From their vantage point beneath a huge old maple, they had a perfect view across the lawn to the far side of the garden. The photographer was busily positioning family members with the bridal party against a backdrop of climbing roses. Wedding guests thronged the plush grass, flagstone patio and walkways. "I think most of the county must be here."

"Along with a lot of politicians from Helena," Dan put in. He pointed at a group near the patio. "That's Governor Attebury with his wife and the couple with them are the Harrises, he's a state senator. I recognized several other state legislators while Charlotte and I were looking for you."

"I suppose it's not surprising," Raine commented, sipping her champagne. It was delicious, fizzy with just the right amount of tartness. "A wedding is an important social occasion and the McClouds are a family with powerful connections."

"Not to mention fabulous taste in champagne," Charlotte quipped. She waved a hand at the garden, patio and house. "Also incredibly rich, obviously. Is this place gorgeous, or what?"

"It certainly is," Raine said, smiling at her friend's uncomplicated enjoyment of the moment. She glanced at Dan; his rough-hewn features held an expression of indulgent adoration as he watched his wife. Charlotte reached up and kissed him, laughing as she rubbed at the pink smear her lipstick left on his tanned cheek.

A wave of loneliness swept Raine. She'd never shared that kind of easy camaraderie with a man other than the brother-sister affection she had with Trey. And no one had ever looked at her with the total love she'd glimpsed in Dan's eyes as he watched Charlotte.

"…don't you think, Raine?"

"I'm sorry, what were you saying?" Raine had no idea what Charlotte was talking about since she hadn't been paying attention.

"I said, I think this wedding is a miracle. First Luke and Rachel got together and now Zach and Jessie—what are the chances that even one Kerrigan and a McCloud would get together, let alone two sets? The odds against it happening twice have got to be astronomical, don't you think?"

"Yes," Raine agreed. "I do." Across the lawn, the photographer was folding his tripod while the family group broke up and trooped toward the patio. "I think the receiving line is about to assemble. Shall we head over there?"

They downed their champagne, handed the empty flutes to a waiter passing by and wound their way through the crowd to join the line of well-wishers. Only a couple of dozen people were queued up ahead of them but by the time Raine reached the bride and groom, the line behind her snaked across the gardens, several hundred guests long.

"Raine." Zach caught her in an exuberant hug, lifting her off her feet. "I wasn't sure you'd make it."

She laughed and hugged him back with equal enthusiasm. "I wouldn't miss your wedding. You told me years ago it would never happen and I had to be here to say, 'I told you so.'"

"That's right. I did say that, didn't I," Zach said wryly. "I made that stupid comment when I was a teenager so I can't be held accountable as an adult, can I?"

"Of course you can," Raine said promptly. "And if I remember correctly, you owe me five dollars for losing the bet. You can pay me when you get back from your honeymoon."

Zach threw his head back and laughed. Beside him, Jessie said goodbye to an elderly woman and turned to slip her arm through his. "What's so funny?" Her warm smile didn't cool when she looked inquiringly at Raine.

"I reminded Zach of a bet we made in high school. He was positive he'd never marry and I was so sure he would."

"I'm glad you won that bet," Jessie said.

"Me, too." Raine felt a rush of emotion. There was a glow about the couple, they seemed to radiate happiness and contentment. "Congratulations to you both. I hope you have many wonderful years together."

"Thank you." Jessie leaned forward

and much to Raine's astonishment, hugged her. "Zach's told me what a good friend you were to him when he was in high school," she said. "I hope you'll come visit us, and soon."

"I, um…thank you," Raine managed to say. "I'll try."

"Congratulations, you two." The deep voice of a rancher behind her interrupted them.

"I'm holding up the line." Raine waggled her fingers in farewell and moved on to the next person in the reception line, steeling herself to face Margaret McCloud. Dressed in a raw silk evening suit, the sapphire tone accentuating her creamy skin and auburn hair, pinned high in a French twist, Chase's mother radiated elegance.

"Raine, how lovely to see you." Margaret captured Raine's hand in both hers. "I'm so glad you could join us today."

"Thank you, Mrs. McCloud. It was a lovely ceremony."

"It was, wasn't it?" Margaret's eyes, the same deep blue as her daughter's, misted. "I love weddings."

Someone jostled Raine and murmured an apology.

"I'm afraid I'm holding up the line," Raine said with a polite smile.

"We'll talk later," Margaret promised. She turned to her husband, standing beside her. "John, I'm sure you remember Raine Harper."

"Of course." Chase's father took Raine's hand from his wife's and like Margaret, enfolded it between his warm, callous-roughened palms. "It's a pleasure to see you, Raine. I understand you and Chase have been working together."

"Yes," Raine said, dazed by the warmth of the McCloud's welcome when she'd been so sure they would barely acknowledge her. "We have."

"I was sorry to hear about your brother's disappearance. Chase will find him, no doubt about it." John's voice held total confidence.

"I think so, too, Mr. McCloud." And she did, Raine realized. She was convinced Chase would find Trey; the only worry she had was how quickly he could make it happen. She wanted it sooner, rather than later.

"Have you tried the champagne, Dad?"

Raine looked over her shoulder. Chase stood directly behind her, holding three full champagne flutes.

"Not since your mother made me sample a glass when the caterer was here a couple of weeks ago." John released Raine's hand and took one of the flutes. "As I recall, it was pretty damn good."

Chase handed one of the flutes to Raine, then reached over her shoulder to give the other one to Margaret. His mother smiled her thanks and sipped appreciatively before turning back to the long line of waiting guests.

"I'm stealing Raine from you, Dad," Chase said, taking her hand.

"All right. Nice to see you, Raine."

John's eyes twinkled and he touched the rim of his flute to hers. "Careful with this stuff. It tastes like smooth, fizzy pale wine but it can sneak up on a person. The worst headache I've ever had was on the morning after Margaret and I drank too much champagne at an inauguration ball."

"I'll keep that in mind, thanks." Raine smiled and let Chase draw her away several steps before she realized they were abandoning the receiving line. "Wait," she murmured, tugging on his hand. "I didn't finish congratulating the wedding party. Zach's mom is there, and the bridesmaids, and the groomsmen…"

"If you really want to talk to each and every one of them, I'll make sure you catch them later. Right now, let's score some food. I'm starving and you'll likely get a screaming headache from the champagne if you don't eat something."

"I'm not sure that's true," she said, trying to remember what she'd eaten earlier in the day. All she could remember downing was a small container of yogurt—she'd been too nervous to eat.

"Trust me. I know these things."

Chase bypassed the crowds at the buffet tables and drew Raine with him down a shadowed walkway around the side of the house. He led her inside. To their right was the kitchen. They dodged hurrying waiters and kitchen staff to reach the counter on the far side. Chase picked up two heavily laden plates covered with clear plastic wrap, hooked an unopened bottle of chilled champagne with two fingers and nodded at the hall door just beyond.

"If you'll get the door, we're outta here."

Raine followed him into another hallway. "Where are we?" She asked as they climbed a short flight of stairs. "More importantly, where are we going?"

"We're going up the back way to the sunroom."

"There's a sunroom? I didn't notice it from the garden."

"We call it the sunroom but it's really a six-sided addition Dad built on the end of the house so Mom can grow flowers in the winter."

Raine walked past him into a dim room.

"Oh, my," she whispered, halting abruptly. The room had six walls, all composed of floor-to-ceiling windows with mesh screens, while the ceiling itself was tinted glass. The thick-leafed limbs of a giant maple tree had been cleverly trimmed to surround and shield the room from below while allowing a panoramic view of the gardens to anyone inside the room. "This is amazing."

"You don't need to whisper, no one can hear us. They can't see us, either."

Potted plants and hanging ferns filled the room with the scent of green, growing things and Raine was drawn to the screened windows. She dropped her purse and shawl on a nearby wicker table, set her half-empty crystal flute next to them and leaned forward to look down at the gardens. "It's like a fairyland with all the lights and lanterns," she said softly.

"It's pretty," Chase agreed, moving to stand behind her. He slipped his arms around her waist and drew her back to rest against him. "My mother loves flowers."

"It shows," Raine murmured. "The roses are amazing."

"Prize-winning," he said. His head lowered, the rough silk of his hair brushing her throat as he trailed lazy kisses over her shoulder. "Did I tell you how much I like this dress?"

"No." Her lashes drifted lower, the lights in the garden below blurring hazily as she gave herself up to the heady intoxication of his lips against her sensitized skin.

"And the earrings…" He nipped her earlobe.

Raine shivered, nerves jumping with anticipation.

"Even better would be the earrings," he went on, tracing the curve of her ear with his lips. "Without the dress."

She turned her head to look up at him.

His mouth moved warmly over hers, seducing her senses. Circling her arms around his neck, she pressed closer, reveling in the hard strength of his body, when muted laughter sounded on the stairs. Startled, she pushed against his shoulders. Chase released her and was at the table pouring champagne when Luke and Rachel entered.

"I knew we'd find you up here," Luke said, carrying a tray piled high with food in one hand and two bottles of champagne in the other.

"I'm sorry, Chase," Rachel laughingly apologized. "I tried to convince him you might not want company."

"Wouldn't matter if you didn't," Luke put in. "Because Mom, Dad, Jessie and Zach are all on their way up."

"The whole wedding party is joining us?" Raine looked over at Chase but he only smiled and lifted his glass in silent salute.

"I think they wanted the family

together for a private toast," Luke said, setting his tray down on the wicker table. "And there's no way we'll have a moment alone downstairs."

Before Raine could comment, the rest of the McClouds joined them, accompanied by the bridesmaids and groomsmen. Zach's mother, Judith, was with the group and she joined Raine at the window, where she'd retreated to sit on the wide ledge and watch the cheerful chaos.

"How are you holding up, Raine?" Judith asked. "I haven't seen you since just after we heard about Trey disappearing."

"I'm better now, actually. Chase is searching for Trey and I'm very encouraged that we'll find him, hopefully soon."

"I'm glad to hear it. I don't know Chase well but Jessie adores him and has absolute confidence in what appears to be an impressive reputation for solving cases and finding people."

"Mom, come stand with Zach and Rowdy while I take your picture," Rachel called, waving a digital camera at Judith. "You too, Raine, join us."

"You go, Judith, it's a family picture," Raine said, laughing when Rowdy raced up to them and grabbed his grandmother's hands to yank her to her feet.

"Bring Raine with you, Mom," Zach called. "In fact, let's see how many of us we can crowd into one photo."

Judith rolled her eyes. "I've never seen my son so happy," she said. "You may as well give in and join us, Raine. Zach won't give up until you do."

Raine would have demurred but Chase set down his champagne and reached her just as Rowdy tugged Judith away. Raine threaded her fingers through his, letting him draw her to her feet.

A burst of laughter at Rowdy's antics made it impossible to be heard. Without considering how her action might look to onlookers, Raine laid her palm against Chase's cheek and turned his head to her with easy familiarity.

He bent toward her in order to hear.

"Are you sure I'm not intruding?" she murmured. "This is obviously a family celebration—I can wait downstairs until you're finished."

"If you leave, I'm going with you." He lifted her hand to his mouth and brushed the backs of her fingers with his lips. "I brought you up here to get away from people, remember?"

"Not to get away from your family," she murmured in protest.

"No," he admitted, smiling faintly. "But stay anyway."

"Are you sure?" She whispered.

"I'm sure."

Reassured, Raine walked beside him to join the group that included Judith, Rowdy, Zach and Jessie. They were quickly caught up in the photographer's insistence that everyone say "broccoli" at the same time. Their efforts failed in four successive attempts, ending in Rowdy's giggles and adult laughter. Raine turned from Rowdy who was making faces at her and caught Zach looking at her with an odd, speculative expression. She mouthed "what" but he shook his head and turned back to face the camera.

Glancing away for a moment while talking with Margaret and John McCloud after the photo session, Raine noticed Zach take Chase aside.

"You'll probably tell me it's none of my business, but I don't see the point in being anything but straight with you," Zach said bluntly.

Chase eyed him over the rim of his glass.

"I know Raine's hired you to look for Trey. I'm guessing you're the best chance she has of locating him, and I'm glad you're helping her."

"But?" Chase said coolly.

"But I've known Raine since she was a kid. She's strong and independent in most areas of her life but she hasn't had a lot of experience with men. Oh, she doesn't have any trouble handling customers at the Saloon or tossing men out on their ear if needed. But she's not a woman who's had a string of lovers."

"And your point is?" Chase would have walked away from the conversation had this been anyone other than Zach. Jessie loved him and Chase had grown to privately acknowledge Zach might be the one man good enough for his little sister. So he stayed, even though he didn't want to hear what Zach was telling him.

"My point is…" Zach looked across the room at Raine. "Be careful with her. I don't want her hurt—she deserves better."

"Yes," Chase said, his somber gaze fixed on Raine. "She does."

Across the room, Raine felt the weight of his stare and looked over her shoulder. Both Chase and Zach were looking at her, their expressions somber.

What's that all about? she wondered, but before she could excuse herself and find out, Margaret McCloud touched her arm, reclaiming her attention.

"I was so glad to learn Chase is helping you search for your brother."

"It was fortunate he had an opening in his schedule," Raine replied.

Margaret's expression was warm and friendly, her gaze compassionate. "Chase is busy," she said. "And he's becoming increasingly involved with running our family properties so I believe he's taking on fewer cases in general. I was glad to hear he'd agreed to work with you, though."

"Really?" Raine was stunned.

"Yes," Margaret said with conviction. "Unless I've misunderstood your situation, you and your twin are the only members of your family remaining. Is that correct?"

Raine nodded, her throat suddenly filled with emotion.

"Then it's even more important that your brother is found, and as quickly as possible." Margaret covered Raine's hand with hers in brief, warm comfort. "A woman needs family about her. And in your particular instance, the missing person is your twin. I'm assuming the two of you are close?"

"Yes, we are. Twins frequently bond

tighter than other siblings," Raine responded. "Trey has always been my best friend, even though he's a guy and not a sister."

Margaret smiled. "I think my daughter considers her brothers very important, too, but she's always struggled with being their 'little sister.' Chase and Luke can be overbearingly protective of her at times."

"Trey gets a little overprotective sometimes, too," Raine said. "I think it must be a guy thing. I've never successfully convinced him to back off if he thought I was making a wrong decision, no matter the subject—whether it was about my job or my dating someone he didn't approve of."

"Do you think he'd approve of your hiring Chase to search for him?" Margaret asked, her voice curious.

"Yes." Raine's response was instant. "Neither of us ever believed Chase had anything to do with Mike's death. In fact, Trey swore on the day of Angus

McCloud's funeral that he'd find a way to prove Chase innocent someday."

Margaret's eyes filled with tears and she drew Raine close in a quick, spontaneous hug.

"Thank you." She released Raine and dabbed at her eyes. "None of us believed the Kerrigans' version of what happened to cause the wreck, either, but it was impossible to disprove the physical evidence."

"You mean that Chase was found unconscious behind the wheel of his truck?"

Margaret nodded but whatever she was about to say was prevented when John McCloud's voice rose above the hum of conversation.

"Sorry, folks, but we'd better head downstairs. Jessie reminded me that Rowdy wants the bride and groom to cut the cake so he can eat it."

In the ensuing bustle as the group cleared the room, Raine and Margaret were separated. Raine was left to wonder what Chase's mother may have said if there had been time and privacy to continue their conversation. She was determined to convince Chase to tell her his version of the long-ago events, and soon.

Chapter Eight

The Wolf Creek Saloon was a popular spot on Saturday nights. Older couples from outlying ranches drove into Wolf Creek for dinner at the restaurant, then went next door to listen to a live band, dance and visit with their neighbors. Younger married couples and singles did likewise, making the Saloon the social club of choice for the town and surrounding area.

Raine said good-night to the restaurant kitchen staff just after closing at

10:00 p.m. and walked down the back hall to the Saloon. She entered just to the left of the long bar, waved to an acquaintance across the noisy, crowded room and took the empty stool next to Charlotte.

"Good crowd tonight," she commented, assessing the number of people present.

"They seem to love this band. Did you book them for next week, too?"

"They're here for a month."

"Excellent."

The two women studied the five-member group occupying the raised bandstand at the end of the room. Couples crowded the dance floor, two-stepping to the band's version of a fast Toby Keith country song.

"I'll be right back." Charlotte touched Raine's shoulder and pointed across the room. "Rocky's waving at me." She slipped off her stool and pushed her way through the crowd toward the bouncer, standing with a waitress next to a table of eight near the door.

"More coffee, boss?"

Raine swung around, smiling at the bartender. "Yes. Thanks, Sam."

"Any news about Trey?" he asked as he poured coffee into her mug.

"Nothing, I'm afraid." Raine saw disappointment and concern furrow the older man's brow and patted his hand. "I know, Sam, I'm worried, too. But I'm convinced Chase will find him—it's just a matter of time."

"I sure hope you're right." Sam's dark eyes were grave. "It's not the same here without him."

"I know," Raine said gently. Sam had worked for the Harper family since she and Trey were preteens and after their parents died, had been a solid rock they'd both leaned on. "I'm glad you're here, Sam. I don't know how I'd keep the businesses running without you."

He shrugged. "I'm just doing my job. You concentrate on finding Trey."

"Hey, Sam…!"

"I'm comin'," he yelled at the rowdy

trio at the far end of the bar, waving empty longnecks at him, before glancing back at her. "You hang in there, Raine. McCloud will find him."

"Thanks, Sam." Raine was convinced that it was only a matter of time before Chase located Trey. *But how much time?* she wondered, impatient for the search to be over, for the uncertainty to end.

A man climbed onto the stool vacated by Charlotte, bumping Raine's shoulder, and she grimaced slightly at the strong scent of expensive cologne mixed with the smell of whiskey.

"Well, well, if it isn't the boss lady. I'm surprised you're working tonight."

Annoyed, Raine turned slowly on her stool.

Lonnie Kerrigan stared at her, a smile on his lips that didn't reach his eyes. He was a younger, heavier version of his father, with the same thick brown hair combed back from his forehead above smooth, handsome features. Like Harlan, he was tall and broad-shouldered, but unlike his father, his good looks were starting to blur under the influence of too much alcohol and rich food. His waist had thickened and a paunch was visible above the expensive silver buckle on his belt.

"I work most nights, Lonnie. I haven't had the…pleasure…of seeing you in the Saloon for months."

His eyes, slightly bloodshot, narrowed at her faint but unmistakable sarcasm. "I've been in Helena, looking after political interests."

Raine wondered if Lonnie meant he'd been bribing someone for his father, or applying muscle to some unfortunate legislator who'd run afoul of Harlan.

"I stopped by last week and the bartender told me you were out of town," Lonnie continued. "Have you found your brother yet?"

"No."

"Maybe you should hire somebody competent. Word is you've got an ex-con working for you."

"Really?" Raine forced a smile. "And who would that be?"

His smile disappeared. "You mean you *didn't* hire McCloud?"

"If you mean Chase McCloud, then yes, I did." She waved a hand dismissively. "But you referred to an ex-con so I assumed you weren't talking about Chase."

"He did jail time. You must remember why," he said sarcastically, "since it was your brother he killed."

"Did he?" Raine's gaze locked with his. "I've never been convinced it was Chase's fault Mike died." She saw with satisfaction that she'd scored a direct hit when his eyes widened briefly.

"Then you're an idiot," he snapped.

"I agree someone certainly is," she said with cool composure.

He visibly restrained himself, his beefy hand closing into a fist atop the bar surface. "It might be smart of you to get rid of McCloud. I thought my father made that clear."

"I'm afraid I don't consult Harlan, or you," she added, "when I decide to hire or fire someone."

He half rose from his stool, looming over her. "Listen, bitch," he growled, grabbing her upper arm in one hand and squeezing painfully, lowering his face to within inches of hers.

She grimaced as his alcohol-scented breath reached her nostrils and his expression turned uglier.

"Let go of her." The command was flat and made more lethal by its lack of emotion.

Lonnie looked over his shoulder at the man standing behind him. He released Raine and straightened.

Raine peered around him, unconsciously rubbing her arm where he'd gripped it.

"Well, I'll be damned," Lonnie said. "McCloud."

"Kerrigan." Chase's ice-blue stare moved past him to flick over Raine, pausing to focus on her upper arm.

Something hot flared in the cold depths of his eyes. "Did he hurt you?"

Raine immediately stopped rubbing her arm. "No."

He looked back at Lonnie. "Don't ever touch her again."

Lonnie ignored Chase's warning as if he hadn't spoken. "I heard you were around, McCloud, but I haven't seen you in town. Folks say you might be avoiding me."

A small, cold smile barely curved Chase's mouth. "Not hardly."

"No? But nobody sees you in Wolf Creek very often. Don't you miss your old friends?"

"I didn't leave anything in this town I cared enough to come back for."

Lonnie's eyes gleamed maliciously as he glanced at Raine. "Maybe that's changed."

"Maybe. All you need to remember is this—you ever touch her again and you'll regret it."

"Big talk." Lonnie's face flushed redder and he stepped away from the bar.

His arms lifted, hands curling into fists as he crouched slightly.

Raine twisted on the stool, searching for Sam. He was standing several feet away and gave her a slight nod, letting her know he'd already pushed the alarm behind the bar. The direct line to the sheriff's office would have already alerted the deputy on duty. She turned back, sweeping the crowd around her with one swift glance. To her relief, no one except for a few people in the immediate vicinity seemed to be aware there was about to be a fight.

Chase stood calmly, watching Lonnie posturing. Dressed in faded jeans, polished black cowboy boots and a white polo shirt with his company logo embroidered over the left pocket, Chase appeared relaxed and faintly amused. Raine was struck by the differences between the two men. Lonnie's heavier torso looked bulky and ungainly compared to Chase's, his alcohol-fueled anger no match for Chase's predatory watchfulness and honed body.

"You plan to actually do something,

Kerrigan, or are you just going to dance around all night?"

He lunged at Chase, throwing a punch that had the potential for serious damage, had it connected. But Chase shifted sideways and Lonnie's fist caught only empty air. With one smooth kick, Chase used Lonnie's forward momentum to knock his feet out from under him and he crashed to the floor.

"Hey! Fight!"

The customers nearest the two combatants scrambled back to clear an open space.

Lonnie got to his feet, cursing. His face was scraped and his lip bleeding from where he'd struck the wooden floor. He swung at Chase again. With smooth efficiency, Chase shifted sideways once more, this time dealing a short, hard blow to Lonnie's chin. Lonnie's head snapped back and his expression reflected dumb surprise just before his eyes rolled upward and he sank to the floor without a sound.

"Well, hell. I would have paid an admission fee to see that and I almost missed it." The quiet satisfaction in the uniformed deputy's voice made onlookers laugh. "Go back to whatever you were doing, folks. The fight's over."

The younger of the two deputies walked to the bar and asked Sam for a pitcher of water. The older deputy looked questioningly at Raine, then at Chase. "I'm guessing Lonnie was being drunk and disorderly? Maybe took an unprovoked punch at you, Chase?"

"Something like that," Chase said evenly. He'd gone to high school with the deputy; they'd played football together, but he hadn't seen or talked to Steve Blake in fifteen years.

"Exactly like that," Raine interjected. "He grabbed me and fortunately, Chase walked in."

"He grabbed you? Are we talking assault charges?" Steve looked hopeful.

Raine glanced at Chase. He gave a little shrug as if to say it was her decision. "No," she said. "He squeezed my arm a little too tight, that's all."

"That's enough for a minor assault complaint."

"I'll be happy just to have him banned from the Saloon," Raine replied. "I think his bar of choice is on the other side of town. He doesn't come in here often so I rarely have to deal with him and I'd like that to continue."

"I'll put that in my notes," Steve said. "I drove out to your place a couple of times in the last few months, Chase, but didn't catch you at home either time."

"I'm away a lot on business," Chase replied.

"Well, don't be such a stranger. Stop by the office sometime and we'll swap war stories about chasing the bad guys." He grinned and held out his hand.

"Sure." Chase shook his hand, off balance at the friendly treatment. He hadn't expected acceptance from anyone who'd been a friend of Mike Harper's, although he didn't recall Steve being part of the high school crowd who'd shunned him after Mike's death.

"Throw the water on him and wake him up, Jim." Steve waved the younger deputy closer. "I don't plan to carry him back to the station."

Raine stepped hastily back and Chase moved next to her, out of the way of splashing water. The deputy emptied the pitcher of cold water on Lonnie's head and he came awake with a roar, sitting up and shaking his head, spraying bystanders.

"Are you ready to get out of here?" Chase murmured, his lips against her ear to be heard above the noise and confusion as customers scrambled away from Lonnie.

"Definitely." She pointed behind him. "Let's go out the back way, through the restaurant."

Raine waved goodbye to Sam and led Chase to the dim hallway beyond.

"Where are we?" he asked, following her.

"This passage connects the restaurant and the Saloon."

They entered the empty, quiet restaurant. Only security lights cast a soft glow along the back wall.

Raine stopped and looked up at him. "Thanks for what you did back there."

"No problem." He cupped her chin in his hand, tilting her face upward to search her eyes. "I meant what I told him. If he comes near you again, I want to know about it."

"You're the first person I'll call."

"Good." His fingers stroked across her cheek, then released her.

"My car's across the street," Raine told him as they stepped out onto the sidewalk. "Do you want to come to my place? I guarantee it's quieter there."

"If I come to your house, I'm staying for breakfast. Are you ready for that?"

"Yes." Raine answered without hesitation, knowing her decision was the right one.

His eyes flared with something dark and hot. "I'm parked near your car. I'll follow you."

Anticipation and excitement warred

with Raine's instinctive need to set ground rules. She thought about it during the drive home, Chase's headlights steady in her rearview mirror.

"I think we need to talk about this," she said, sidestepping him when he would have pulled her into his arms the moment the door closed behind them.

"You want to talk?" Surprise laced his voice.

"There are a few things I want to make clear." She took his hand and led him down the dark hallway to her bedroom.

"All right." Amusement replaced surprise; he trailed his lips over her fingers before turning her hand over and pressing a hot, open mouthed kiss against her palm.

"I don't want you to think I sleep around."

"Why would I think that?"

"Well, in case you do…I want to make it clear, I don't sleep around. I don't have time, for one thing. I'm busy with the restaurant and it takes a lot of my time, plus there's the motel. And if Trey's not here, then I have to manage the Saloon, too."

"Okay."

"That is why I need time to think about this…and us."

"Right."

"Because I don't do casual sex."

"Uh-huh." He unbuttoned her blouse, the backs of his fingers brushing down the valley between her breasts to her midriff.

"I'm serious." He reached the sensitive skin just above her navel and she sucked in her breath, her skin quivering beneath the stroking of his warm fingers.

"Are you trying to tell me you're a virgin?"

"What? No! Of course not. I've had sex before." Her cheeks burned.

"When?"

"When what?"

"When was the last time you had sex?" he asked patiently, tugging her blouse free from her skirt.

"I don't remember," she confessed.

He stopped, her blouse off her shoulders and halfway down her arms. "You don't remember?" he repeated. "Because it was so long ago? Or because it was so forgettable?"

"Probably both." Raine lifted her head and looked into his eyes. "I told you I don't sleep around."

"Yeah," he said softly. "You did." His gaze holding hers, he released her blouse. It slid down her arms, catching briefly on her wrists before slipping to the floor. He smoothed his palms up her arms to cup her shoulders, then slowly tugged her pink satin bra straps lower until they slipped off her shoulders. He bent his head and kissed her neck, just below her ear.

His warm mouth sent heat curling in her belly and lower.

"Neither do I." He said the words against the base of her throat where her pulse pounded.

"Hmm?" She couldn't think with the thudding of her heartbeat loud in her ears.

"I don't sleep around."

She gazed at him through half-lowered lashes. "You don't?"

"I'm not a virgin." A slow smile curved his mouth, "But I don't do casual sex, haven't since I was a teenager."

"Oh." She tried to think about what he was telling her, what the words might mean. "How long has it been?"

"Long enough." He bent closer, his heated gaze holding hers while he slowly, thoroughly, licked her lower lip. "Are we done talking?" His voice was a low, raspy growl.

She could barely think, let alone form words. She slid her arms around his neck and kissed him. That kiss held all the pent-up longing and desire that had been simmering between them for weeks.

She murmured when he eased away from her to tug her bra free and drop it on the floor. She tugged at the hem of his shirt and he pulled it off over his head, tossing it behind him as she pressed eagerly against him, sleek skin and lush curves naked against his. He groaned and took her mouth, his hands closing over her bottom to lift her higher while his mouth ravished hers.

He caught a handful of her skirt and tugged it up, the material pooling around his wrist until his hand met bare thigh.

"How does this come off," he muttered, searching for a zipper.

"Just pull."

He tugged, she wriggled, and the skirt slid past her waist and hips to the floor. With one swift motion, he stripped her pink lace undies down her legs to join her skirt before he picked her up and laid her on the bed. Without releasing her, he settled on top of her, mouths fused, his hands stroking the bare, satiny skin of her thighs and the inward curve of her waist. Heat bloomed feverishly everywhere he touched.

She murmured, frantic to have him closer, and slid her palms over his back, down to the waist of his jeans. Frustrated with the denim, she pushed at his chest and he lifted.

"What?" he muttered, one hand cupping her breast, fingers smoothing over the stiff peaks and making her shudder.

"Your jeans...take them off." She fumbled with the metal snap and managed to free it, but the second snap eluded her.

Without a word, he left the bed and toed off his boots. He stripped off his jeans and shorts in one movement, paused to take a packet from his pocket and returned, blanketing her once more.

Raine gasped at the feel of hot, aroused male, naked against her own bare body. She was beyond thinking, driven by the need to have him finish what they'd started. She wrapped her arms around him, drawing him closer.

"Please," she breathed.

He lifted away from her, sheathed himself, and she caught her breath when he nudged, heavy and insistent, against her. She shuddered and gasped when he pushed home and went still, hot and pulsing inside her.

"Don't move," he grated, the muscles

in his arms shaking with the effort. "Give me a minute."

But Raine was beyond comprehending. She lifted against him and he swore softly before setting a rhythm that quickly drove them both over the edge.

"I'm sorry," Raine murmured when she could breathe again.

She lay sprawled across his chest. One of his big hands stroked idly across her bottom while the other was tangled in her hair.

"For what?" he asked, tugging her hair until she looked up at him.

"You asked me not to move. I couldn't stay still."

The lazy smile that lifted the corners of his mouth was filled with satisfaction. "That's all right. You can make it up to me."

"Really? How?"

"Next time you can't move at all until I tell you to."

"Hmm. That sounds like torture—and fun."

"Could be," he acknowledged. "Let's test it."

He rolled her beneath him and took her mouth with his.

Hours later, Raine lay in his arms, moonlight slanting through the window and across the bed.

"Tell me what happened the night Mike died, Chase." She tilted her head back to look up at him, her hair spilling across his bare shoulder. His muscles tensed and she smoothed her palm over his chest. "I know you don't talk about it and I promise I'll never ask again, but I need to know."

"It won't change anything," he warned her. "We can't go back and rewrite history."

"I know," she murmured. "But we lost more than Mike that night. Trey and I lost you, too. I want to understand as much as possible about what happened."

Chase threaded his fingers through her hair and kissed her.

"There wasn't a moon that night," he began. "I'd dropped my date at her place after a movie and was on my way home just before midnight. About five miles from the Kerrigan ranch, my headlights picked up a man, staggering along the edge of the road. I thought he might be hurt and I pulled up behind him and stopped, left the engine running and got out. He started to turn around, lost his balance and fell face-first into the ditch. I didn't know it was Lonnie until I got him out. He was dead drunk. Said his girlfriend pushed him out of the car because he was drunk and then drove off and left him. I was tempted to leave him there but it was late and pitch-dark—I was afraid he'd do something stupid, like walk down the middle of the road and get run over. So I managed to shove him inside the passenger side of the pickup."

He paused, his fingers tightening in Raine's hair.

"It was a mistake. Before I could walk around the truck and get in on the driver's side, Lonnie slid beneath the wheel and put it in gear. He drove forward several feet and stopped just long enough for me to reach the door, then he drove off again laughing like an idiot.

"The second time he did it, I jumped in the bed of the truck, thinking I could reach him through the cab's open rear sliding window. But he started weaving across the road, trying to throw me out of the back of the truck and keep me from grabbing the keys out of the ignition. I had my head, shoulders and one arm through the window and inside the cab when we topped a hill and saw oncoming headlights.

"I yelled at Lonnie to stop but it was too late. He swerved sideways but the truck clipped the other car and we left the road. I remember sailing out of the back of the truck and hitting the ground a couple of times but then everything went black. When I woke up, I was in the hospital in Wolf Creek. The cops told me I was found behind the wheel of my wrecked truck."

"But how could that be?" Raine asked, riveted by the brief recital and Chase's unemotional voice. "How did you get behind the wheel?"

"That's the question, isn't it. I know what happened before we hit Mike. I have no recollection between the impact and waking up in the hospital. Someone had to have moved Lonnie out from behind the wheel and put me in the truck. There's only one person I know who could have done it."

"Harlan," Raine breathed.

"That's my guess."

"But was he there?"

"I'm convinced he was, but I can't prove it."

"No wonder you hate the Kerrigans," Raine said softly.

"They aren't my favorite people," he admitted. He pulled her closer, stroking a hand over the curve of her bare hip. "Are we finished with the subject? Because I can think of a lot of things I'd rather be doing with you than talking about old history."

"We're finished." *For now*, she thought.

Raine lost track of the number of times they made love before they fell asleep, exhausted and limbs entangled, just as the eastern sky began to lighten with rosy dawn.

They slept in, and Raine didn't get to work until nearly noon the following day. Charlotte lifted her eyebrows but Raine merely smiled sunnily and sidestepped her friend's questions. She was at her desk, going over the prior day's bookkeeping for the restaurant when someone pushed wide the half-open door.

"Chase." She was delighted to see him, in fact, she'd been daydreaming about him since she'd arrived at the office. The hot memories weren't conducive to finishing paperwork.

He stepped into the office, his face grim and her welcoming smile faded. "What is it? What's wrong?"

"I just came from the sheriff's office. Some kids out target shooting in a rancher's gravel pit found Trey's SUV."

Raine's heart pounded with dread. "Is he…"

"He wasn't with the vehicle."

The room teetered and Chase slipped out of focus, his outline blurring for a moment. "I want to see it."

"I'll drive you."

As she stood, her knees buckled and she swayed, catching herself with a hand on the edge of the desk. Chase reached her in three long strides. He wrapped his arms around her, tucking her against him while one big hand cradled the back of her head.

Raine shuddered, her arms circling him and her hands gripping the back of his shirt. "Oh, Chase…" she got out, her voice trembling.

"It's okay, honey." His deep voice calmed her. "This doesn't mean he's not alive."

She burrowed against the solid strength of his body. His heat warmed the coldness that filled her and the shivers that shook her slowly ceased.

At last, Raine released his shirt and

tipped her head back to look up at him. He cupped her cheek, smoothing his thumb over the damp tracks of tears to dry them.

"The sheriff hasn't moved the vehicle yet. Are you sure you want to go out there? We can wait until it's towed in."

"No, I want to see the place where it was found. Is the site near the highway?"

He nodded. "About sixty miles east of here and a little north."

"East and north?" She frowned in confusion. "But Billings is straight south of Wolf Creek. Why would Trey have been driving in the opposite direction?"

"That's one of the things we need to find out."

"All right." She stepped back and drew a deep breath. "I'm ready."

His gaze searched her face. Apparently satisfied with what he saw, he settled a supportive, possessive hand on her waist and they left the office.

In less than an hour, Chase eased his black SUV off the highway and through an open ranch gate. A Sheriff's Department patrol car was parked just inside and the deputy on guard waved them on. They bumped over an ungraded dirt road that wound around a hill, climbing upward until they topped the rise. Below them was a scooped-out area the size of a small football stadium with rock and gravel piled haphazardly along one side. Halfway across the open area, two sheriff's vehicles, a red pickup and a tow truck were parked next to a dirty silver SUV.

A dust cloud spiraled skyward behind their wheels as Chase drove down the winding track and across the gravel pit over to the cluster of vehicles.

The four men standing next to the tow truck turned to look when Chase parked behind them. One of them was a uniformed sheriff's deputy and he left the group to approach Chase and Raine as they got out.

"Afternoon, folks. Are you Raine Harper and Chase McCloud?"

"That's right. You must be Deputy Skinner?" Chase asked.

"Yes. My sergeant told me to hold the vehicle here until you two arrived and had a chance to look at it." He jerked his thumb toward the dusty SUV. "Not much to see, I'm afraid. I understand the owner is listed as missing so the lab boys will go over it more thoroughly when we tow it in, but there aren't any obvious signs of foul play."

"Is it unlocked?" Chase asked.

The deputy nodded. "We found the keys on the gravel heap over there." He pointed to a huge mound of rough gravel a few yards away. "I'm guessing whoever abandoned the SUV drove it here, tossed away the keys, then got in a second car and left."

"Sounds reasonable. We'll take a look at the vehicle now, if that's all right."

"Sure. As soon as you're done, I'll tell the tow truck driver he can hook up and move it."

"We shouldn't be too long." Chase let Raine step ahead of him.

Raine felt his solid presence, one pace behind her, as she walked toward the

SUV. She was grateful he'd let her go first, giving her time.

He stopped when they were several feet from the SUV and waited, hands tucked into his jeans pockets while he watched her.

While walking around the SUV she noticed that the back right taillight was broken and the bumper dented below, as if the driver had backed into something. Dried mud coated the tires and the wheel wells.

The driver's door was ajar and she climbed inside. The interior was cluttered with empty fast-food cartons, candy wrappers and used soda cans.

"Don't touch anything. We wouldn't want to destroy fingerprints for the lab," Chase said quietly. "Are you getting any vibes?"

Deep in reflection, Raine startled, her heart beating wildly faster. She pressed her palm to her chest and drew a calming breath. "No." She gestured at the dirty interior. "Trey would have a fit if he saw this—he keeps his vehicle scrupulously clean."

Leaning in, Chase peered at the passenger seat and carpeted floor, littered with trash. "They were slobs."

He made the statement with such matter-of-fact conviction that Raine smiled. "I've been in your car and given its pristine condition, I'm guessing you and Trey are of the same opinion about keeping your vehicles spotless."

"If you mean your brother would agree with me about his SUV having been trashed by slobs, then you're right." He touched her shoulder briefly and straightened. "Let me know when you're done in here." He left to examine the front of the vehicle.

"Ma'am?" Deputy Skinner drew Raine's attention away from Chase.

"Yes?"

"I'll have to ask you not to touch anything. I'm stretching the limits by allowing you inside the vehicle."

"Thanks, Deputy." Raine slid out of

the driver's seat, careful not to touch anything as she did so. "I appreciate your letting us do this much."

"Yes, ma'am." He moved back several feet to wait.

Raine surveyed the dirty front of the vehicle. She wasn't sure what she hoped to see—she'd been so convinced that she would feel something from Trey here. He'd been driving the SUV when he left home for Billings. Surely there would be some clue here—if not inside the vehicle, then perhaps outside.

Chase was hunkered on his heels, carefully inspecting the right rear tire.

"Did you find something?" Raine asked, kneeling beside him.

"Maybe." He pointed at the tire. "This tire isn't as worn as the others. I'm guessing it might be the spare. Do you know if Trey had a flat and put this on before he disappeared?"

She shook her head. "Not that I know of—if he did, he didn't mention it."

"The other interesting thing is the mud on the tires and the wheel wells."

Raine looked at the clumps of reddish mud coating the wheel well and smeared on the tires. "It just looks like mud to me."

"Ah, but it's mixed with clay. I've only seen this kind of mud in one location."

"Really?" Hope raced through Raine. "Where?"

"About fifty miles farther north. My dad used to take my brother and me pheasant hunting there when we were kids."

"So we have a new clue and a starting point to begin searching again?"

"It's certainly worth looking into," Chase said. He pushed to his feet. "Are you done here?"

"Yes." Raine shifted, wincing as the gravel dug into her knee. "I thought surely I'd feel something when I sat in Trey's car, but I haven't…" She braced the flat of her palm on the tire to push upright. "Oh!" She snatched her hand away in shock, cradling it against her midriff.

"What?" Chase demanded. "Are you all right?"

"The tire," she said softly, staring at it.

"What's wrong with it?" Chase frowned, uncomprehending.

"Trey changed the tire that night. And something bad happened to him when he did."

Chase knelt beside her, taking her hands in his. "How bad?" His eyes were grim as he searched her face.

"He's hurt."

"But not dead?" Chase asked.

She shook her head, her hair swinging forward to brush her cheeks. "No. But I think whoever stole this car harmed Trey." She clutched his fingers. "We need to find him, Chase."

"We will." He helped her to her feet, tucking her beneath his arm and took her back to his car. "I'll be right back."

He crossed the uneven ground to Deputy Skinner and exchanged a few words before the two shook hands. Then he rejoined Raine.

"Where to now?" she asked.

He glanced at his watch and shifted into gear. "Now I take you home and head north."

"I want to go with you."

"Your choice. By the time we drive home, pick up Killer and pack bags it's going to be late. We might as well start early tomorrow morning. How long can you be away from the Saloon and restaurant?"

"As long as I need to."

He nodded, glancing at her before he took her hand and placed it palm down on his thigh, covering it with his.

"We'll find him, Raine. I promise."

Chapter Nine

They left Wolf Creek before eight the following morning, driving straight through to the northern county Chase had visited on those boyhood hunting trips with his father and Luke.

They spent a long day repeating their earlier pattern of stopping at each truck stop, mini-mart and town along the highway to ask questions and show residents Trey's photo. But when they checked into a motel after 9:00 p.m., they had nothing to show for their day except a higher mileage reading on Chase's speedometer.

Raine kicked off her sandals and combed her fingers through her hair. "I'm going to shower and climb into bed. I'm exhausted."

"Go ahead. I need to check my messages." Chase dialed as she unzipped her bag and took out a light tank top and sleeping shorts. "You can skip the pajamas, honey," he drawled, amused when she flushed. "I'll just take them off again."

Distracted by the sway of her hips as she marched into the bathroom, he nearly missed the first message.

"…Steve Blake with the sheriff's office. Just wanted to let you know—we got a hit on the fingerprints found in Trey's abandoned SUV. They belong to Carl and Bobby Rimes. You probably remember them—they were a few years ahead of us in school. They've both got rap lists as long as my arm. And get this—they've been employed on Harlan Kerrigan's ranch for the last ten months. We've sent out a state-wide bulletin to all law enforcement agencies to arrest and transfer them back here if they're apprehended. I'll let you know if we get any further information."

The message ended.

The men who carjacked Trey worked for Harlan? Chase had his own reasons for disliking Harlan and he knew the man was capable of anything. But would he have reason to harm Trey?

Raine had commented earlier today that she'd planned to accompany Trey the night he disappeared, but had fallen ill. They'd argued when she'd insisted on going with him, despite a fever that spiked her temperature to 101 degrees, and later that evening, her brother had slipped out without her.

Chase's blood had chilled when he realized how close she'd come to disappearing along with Trey.

If there was a possibility Harlan

Kerrigan might be involved, Raine was still in danger.

Driven by the need for reassurance she was safe, he dropped the phone on the bedside table and stripped off his shirt as he entered the bathroom. Steamy and humid, the room smelled like her floral-scented soap. It took only seconds for Chase to unbutton his jeans and shove them and his shorts down his legs.

The plastic curtain rings jingled when he pulled it aside and stepped into the shower.

Raine glanced over her shoulder and smiled. "Hi."

"Come here." He slipped his arms around her waist and pulled her against him. Her bare body was slippery and wet, the showerhead pelting them with warm water. He kissed her and she opened her mouth, welcoming the thrust of his tongue, rising on tiptoe to wrap one slim leg around his and pull him nearer.

The cove of her thighs cradled his

erection. He caught her waist and lifted her higher.

"Wrap your legs around me," he muttered, trying to slow down and give her time to catch up with him. But she complied so quickly he forgot his good intentions and thrust into her, unable to stop, shuddering with the effort to not move. "Are you okay?"

"Yes," she breathed against his mouth. "Don't stop. Please."

Reassured, Chase pinned her against the tiled wall and drove them both over the edge. Long moments later, he set her on the bathmat and tenderly dried her before picking her up and carrying her to bed.

They made love once more before he tucked her close, her back to his chest, the smooth length of her legs tangled with his. His palm cupped her breast, his arm at her waist, soothing his need to feel her, safe and vibrantly alive against him.

"Thank you," she murmured sleepily.

"For what?"

"For being you. For being here."

"My pleasure."

By midafternoon the next day, Raine was growing more discouraged with each stop.

"Don't give up," Chase advised as·they drove away from a gas station on the outskirts of a tiny town. "There's a long list of places we haven't been yet and a longer list of potential witnesses to check. What's the next stop?"

She took the map from the seat divider and studied it. "A small town about fifteen miles ahead."

They got off the highway twenty minutes later to drive into Granger, a small ranching community, and parked in front of what appeared to be a combination of bar and restaurant.

Raine shaded her eyes against the hot sunlight, scanning the front of the establishment. The facade was freshly painted, the windows and glass door of the restaurant clean, the sidewalks swept and neat. Everything about the outward appearance spoke of pride of ownership.

"Whoever owns this place takes good care of it," she commented as Chase joined her on the sidewalk.

Nothing about the well-kept buildings seemed out of the ordinary. Yet Raine's heart suddenly beat faster, her muscles tightening in anticipation.

"What is it, Raine?"

"I'm not sure." Instinctively, she moved toward the bar entrance.

They paused just inside. The tables and booths were empty but two women were at the bar. The older woman, seated on a stool, ignored them, lifting her glass to drink.

The younger woman stood behind the bar, drying glassware. "Good morning," she said cheerfully. "Come in and have a seat."

Raine's heart was pounding so loudly in her ears that she could barely hear the words. Chase took her hand, threading his fingers through hers. The action steadied her. Each step she took as they crossed the room heightened her anticipation.

"What can I get you?" The bartender asked as they sat.

"Just coffee." Chase drew the photo of Trey from his pocket and laid it on the bar. "And a little information."

"What kind of information?" The slim blonde filled two mugs and set them on the bar in front of them.

The older woman seated two stools beyond Chase stiffened, abruptly set down her drink and leaned forward to look at the picture.

"We're looking for this man." Chase slid the photo across the polished bar surface. "Have you seen him?"

The blonde's eyes widened and her face paled. "Yes." She looked up at Chase. "I have."

"When?" Raine couldn't keep silent. "Where?"

Before she could answer, a loud crash interrupted them.

"Damn." A man stepped into the room, carrying a large carton. "Sorry, Lori. I knocked over the recycling bin again."

"Trey." Raine swayed, catching Chase's arm for support.

Her brother froze, staring at her. He wore a black T-shirt and jeans and his dark hair was a shade too long. Beard stubble shadowed his face, blurring the lines of cheekbones and jaw. "You're the woman in my dreams," he said slowly.

The blonde caught her breath. "You dreamed about her?"

Raine registered the trace of pain beneath the words and glanced at her in time to see recognition and wonder drawn on her expressive features.

"You two look so much alike—the same eyes…"

"We're twins," Raine said. She gazed wordlessly at the beloved lines of Trey's face. The unfamiliar black stubble and longer hair altered his appearance but it didn't matter. She'd recognize Trey in total darkness simply by the feeling of completeness and peace that filled her. "We've been looking for you."

"Have you? I wondered if I'd been missed somewhere." Trey turned to set the box down on the table.

Raine gasped. "You've been hurt. What happened?"

He brushed his fingertips over an angry-looking red scar on his right temple, just at his hairline. "Well, that's the strange thing. I don't know."

"You don't know?" Chase said with deceptive mildness. "Or you don't remember."

Trey shrugged. "Same thing."

"Not always."

Raine listened to their exchange with growing horror. "You don't remember, do you? Do you know who I am, Trey?"

"Not exactly."

"Do you know who *you* are?" Chase asked.

"That's a loaded question," he answered. "Few people know who they really are."

"You don't know," Raine said, with growing confusion. "No matter. Your name is Trey Harper and you're my brother." She pointed to the angry red scar. "Did you receive a blow to the head when you got that? If so, you could easily have amnesia." She leaned closer. "Look at me—really look at me. We're twins. We have the same color eyes, the same bone structure."

"Seems obvious to me." The woman sitting beyond Chase put in. "The two of you are alike as two peas in a pod. Except one of you is male and the other female." She leaned forward. "I think it's safe to tell your sister what you know."

"Mother…" the blonde protested.

"It's all right, Lori." Trey joined her behind the bar, stroking his palm soothingly over her shoulder. "Your mother's right. I don't see any harm in telling my sister…" He broke off, eyeing Raine quizzically. "I remember your face, but not your name."

"It's Raine. And this is Chase McCloud."

"This is Lori Ashworth and her mother, Risa," Trey said after he and Chase shook hands. "They own the bar and the restaurant next door."

Lori managed a strained smile. Risa, however, tapped her long red fingernails on the bar and surveyed them assessingly.

"Chase McCloud? Even in our little town, we've heard of the McCloud family and Wolf Creek. I admit, when our boy here walked in a few weeks ago and told us he didn't remember his name or much of anything else, I doubted whether it was true. I even wondered if he was running a scam of some sort. But now that you've identified him, well… It's not likely he would have voluntarily left Wolf Creek to work for us in little old Granger, now is it?" She gave a calculating smile. "Is there a reward for keeping him safe?"

"Mother!" Lori groaned.

"I hadn't thought about it." Raine met Trey's gaze, looking for guidance, but couldn't read his expression. "I believe I'll leave that up to my brother since only he knows how safe he's been."

"We'll talk about it later," Trey said.

Risa shrugged. "Can't blame a woman for trying." She gestured meaningfully at Raine. "I still think you should tell her what you told us when you staggered in here that first day."

"Yes," Raine agreed, anxious to hear the details. "Please do."

Before Trey could respond, two cowboys entered and took seats farther down the bar.

"Why don't you move to a table so you can talk without being overheard," Lori suggested. "I'll deal with the customers."

"Come with us. Jeannie can take over for a few minutes." Trey leaned past her to push a call button next to the cash register.

"I'll take their order while we're waiting for her." Lori made shooing gestures at Trey behind her back as she greeted the cowboys.

It took a few moments to regroup at a round table across the room, far enough from the bar for private conversation. Lori soon joined them, her replacement chatting with the older couple who now sat with the cowboys at the long bar.

"There's not much to tell," Trey began. "I woke up along the highway one morning a few weeks ago. There was a lump and a cut on my head and I couldn't remember my name nor where I lived. A trucker gave me a ride as far as Granger and I staggered into the bar where Lori and Risa took pity on me. They cleaned me up, let me use a vacant apartment upstairs, and gave me a job here."

"Did you see a doctor?" Raine asked, frowning at the thin scar on his temple.

"Yeah. He took a couple of stitches, gave me some painkillers and told me not to worry about my memory—said in his experience, most cases like mine resolved themselves within a few weeks."

"And has it? Begun to resolve itself, I mean." Raine studied his face, trying to read his expression.

"I remember bits and pieces," he said vaguely. "Like tending bar and a killer recipe for nachos."

Raine laughed "With jalapenos?"

"So hot it burns all the way down," he agreed, grinning.

"It's one of your specialties at home," she said softly, smiling.

"So the doctor was right," Chase commented. "You're starting to remember."

"Apparently."

Around them, the tables and booths were quickly filling with the after-work crowd of regulars. Behind the bar, Jeannie gestured frantically, claiming Lori's attention.

She shoved her chair back and stood. "It was lovely meeting you, Raine—and Chase—but I'm afraid I have to get back to work."

"Me, too." Trey said as they all rose. "Are you staying in Granger tonight?"

Raine blinked, taken aback. "Uhmm, why... Yes."

"Good. My shift doesn't end until midnight—maybe we can get together for breakfast tomorrow?"

"Of course." She reached blindly for Chase's hand and his fingers closed comfortingly around hers.

"Can you recommend a local hotel?" Chase asked.

"Granger only has one," Lori answered. "Reed's Inn, on the outskirts of town near the highway exit."

"Thanks." Chase touched the brim of his hat and turned Raine toward the door.

She didn't speak until they were in the car and driving toward the motel. "He doesn't know me. If he has amnesia, will he eventually recover?"

"I'm guessing the answer's yes, but I'm not a doctor."

They checked into the motel and ate a late dinner at the café next door, Raine merely picking at her food, before returning to their room.

"If Trey doesn't want to come home, do I have to respect his wishes and walk away?"

"I don't know, honey. I can't imagine any man giving up what Trey has in Wolf Creek to stay here."

"I don't understand any of this."

"Me, either. But you felt something bad, cause unknown, happened to him when you touched his abandoned vehicle. Maybe he remembers enough about whatever happened to be worried his attackers will come looking for him if they know he survived."

"You mean someone might be trying to kill him?" The mere thought terrified Raine.

"Hard to say. All of this is pure speculation until we have more information."

Raine climbed into bed to lie curled against Chase's side, only partially listening to the suspense plot unfolding on the TV screen. She couldn't concentrate on anything except Trey and how they could convince him they were telling him the truth. What if he wouldn't accept her assurances as to his identity? Could she have lost him forever?

Someone knocked on the door. Startled, Raine looked at Chase.

"I'll get it." He picked up his handgun from the bedside table and stood, tucking the gun into the waistband of his jeans at the small of his back. He'd put on only jeans after their shower and the lamplight played across the sleek, honed muscles of his torso as he crossed the room.

Raine sat upright, legs crossed, watching with apprehension as Chase peered through the peephole.

He opened the door and Trey stepped inside quickly, glancing back over his shoulder.

"I might have been followed," he said. "But I don't think so."

"Why would someone be following you?"

"I don't know."

Chase didn't visibly react to the blunt answer, merely nodding at the small round table and chairs in the corner of the room. "Have a seat." He glanced at Raine, including her.

She uncurled from the bed and went over to the table, aware that Trey watched her, his expression unfathomable. He wore the same black T-shirt and jeans he'd had on earlier and she recognized the distinctive, custom-made boots on his feet.

"You ordered those boots from a shop in Dallas," she told him. "They were custom-made and the boot maker stamped your initials, TH, in the tool work just above the ankle on the inside of each boot."

Startled, he stared at her before thrusting his hand through his hair. "Damn. You're right." He pulled out a chair and straddled it, a deep frown creasing his brow. "After you left the bar, I borrowed my boss's office computer and ran a search on your name. You're listed as the owner of a business in Wolf Creek, together with a brother named Trey."

"But you still don't remember Raine or your life in Wolf Creek," Chase said.

"I've been having flashes, bits and pieces of memories, but I don't have a whole picture yet."

"Maybe it would be easier if you told us what you *do* remember and we can fill in the blanks," Chase suggested, looking questioningly at Raine.

She nodded. "That might take less time."

"I have no clear memory of a life prior to roughly three or four weeks ago," Trey began, "when I woke up in a ditch along a highway about thirty miles north and east of here."

"We were searching south of Wolf Creek toward Billings, no wonder we couldn't find you," Raine said.

"You've been looking for me?"

"Yes, constantly. Every day since you disappeared."

"That's good to hear, because I didn't know a soul and felt totally alone. Except for these flashes when it felt like I was being swamped with someone else's emotions, mostly sad."

He smiled and Raine's heart twisted. She hadn't known if she'd ever see that smile again and she wanted to throw her arms around him and hug him tight. But there was a certain distance about him that held her back.

"It might have been me," she said softly. "We're twins and sometimes, we feel what the other one is thinking."

"Really?" He looked intrigued.

"How did you end up here?" Chase prompted.

"This town's postmark was on an envelope I found. I didn't have any ID on me, no wallet, no car keys, nothing to tell me who I was or where I lived."

"But you had an envelope. Didn't it have your address?" Chase asked.

"The address wasn't readable," Trey said. "I woke up facedown in a muddy ditch. When I got up, the envelope was in the water where I'd been lying. The only legible information on it was the postmark, Granger, Montana. All that was left of the address was smears of blue ink. To tell you the truth, I wasn't even sure the letter belonged to me. For all I knew, it could have been trash thrown out of someone's car and left in the ditch for months. But it was the only thing I had."

"Do you still have it?" Chase asked.

"Yeah, back in my room."

"Was there a letter in the envelope?"

"If you could call it that. It was odd. In fact—" he looked at Raine "—any chance I'm being blackmailed? Because the wording of the letter is weird."

"What did it say?" Raine knew because she'd read it herself, but she wanted Trey to tell Chase in his own words.

"I can't give you the exact wording, but it basically told me to meet someone at the Bull 'n' Bash if I wanted to know what really happened fifteen years ago." He shook his head in frustration. "I've been running computer checks but haven't turned up any information on a place called Bull 'n' Bash in Montana or any neighboring state."

"It's a bar in Billings," Chase said. "It's not the kind of place to be online with a Web site. You were on your way there to meet whoever wrote the letter on the night you disappeared."

Trey was silent for a moment, digesting this. "So what do you think happened? Somebody didn't want me to meet the letter writer?"

"We don't know," Raine put in. "That might be true. But it also could be you were hijacked by unconnected persons who simply wanted your vehicle."

"My car's that nice?" Trey grinned, his eyes crinkling at the corners. "I've been without wheels ever since I woke up in that ditch. Good to know I've got a car somewhere."

"You drive a very nice silver SUV," Raine told him. "It was recovered quite a ways south of here just a few days ago. In fact, that's what led us here."

"Really? Why?"

"The wheel wells and tires had red clay soil on them," Chase responded. "That kind of soil isn't common so we changed our search to include the area where it's found."

"Damn." Trey looked impressed. "Good sleuthing, Sherlock."

Chase laughed.

"So, what do we do now? Are you ready to go home?" Raine asked hopefully.

"I have to talk to someone tonight and explain what's going on but, yeah, I'll go back. When are you two leaving?"

"Tomorrow morning, but if you need longer," Chase met Raine's gaze, "we'll wait."

"Tomorrow's good for me." He rose. "Does it work for you to pick me up at the bar around ten tomorrow morning?"

"Absolutely." Chase and Raine stood, too.

Trey shook Chase's hand, pausing to look at Raine.

"Be careful," she murmured and hugged him. He hesitated before hugging her back, patting her shoulder awkwardly.

Then he was gone.

Chase pulled her into his arms, tilting his head to search her face. "Mission accomplished. How do you feel?"

"Relieved. Delighted. So very, very glad to see him, hold him, and know he's alive and well," she said, smiling through tears. "But I'm a little worried about the situation. Why does he seem to feel he's being watched or followed? I meant to ask him and forgot in the excitement. Did you get the feeling there's something else he's not telling us?"

"I think there's more here than meets the eye. But I'm not sure whether it's good to press him too hard for details until he sees a doctor. I don't know a lot about amnesia or what the treatment is to correct it, nor what we should or shouldn't be asking or telling him about the parts of his life he doesn't remember."

"Me, either," Raine confessed. "I can't

wait to get him home and have him see our regular doctor. I'll feel much better once we have an expert examine him and find out if there was any other damage that needs treating besides the scar—like concussion, or a possible fracture."

"You'll have him home by tomorrow afternoon, honey." Chase kissed the end of her nose. "You're such a mother hen."

He waited until she fell asleep before he eased his arm from beneath her head and slipped out of bed. Carrying his cell phone into the bathroom so Raine wouldn't hear him, he eased the door shut and dialed using the phone's slight screen light.

"Yeah?" Ren's voice was raspy with sleep.

"It's Chase."

"What's up?" The words were clearer, more aware. "Do you know what time it is?"

"Late."

"Hell, yes, it's late. This better be important, McCloud."

"It is. I need Andy in Wolf Creek to

guard Raine Harper for a week or two, maybe longer."

"You got it. Anything else?"

"I want you to run a background check on Harlan Kerrigan's activities in Helena, including his personal life."

Ren was silent for a long moment. Chase could hear the faint scratch of pen on paper.

"I'm guessing you're not looking for evidence he's a nice guy, right?"

"I know he's not a nice guy. I want proof he's stepped over the line. I don't care if he's bribed a politician, skimmed profits from his company, had an illegitimate kid or slept with a married woman." Chase gave Ren a quick rundown on Trey's carjacking and assault. "It's bad enough if Harlan targeted Trey but Raine was supposed to be with him that night. She only stayed home because she was ill. I'm going after the Rimes brothers tomorrow but in case I don't get them, I need a back-up plan. Harlan had political ambitions. If we can dig up evidence that implicates him in any scandal, I can use it to threaten him and force him to stay away from the Harpers."

"Until you find real evidence to put him away?" Ren asked.

"That would be the best of all worlds," Chase said grimly.

"I'll call Andy and start researching Kerrigan as soon as I hang up."

"You'll need someone on the ground in Helena. I've kept a file on Harlan for years and never found anything but small-time stuff."

"I'll go myself."

"Thanks."

"Anytime. And Chase…"

"Yeah?"

"I expect an invitation to the wedding."

"You're on the list," Chase said dryly.

Chase rang off with Ren's laughter still echoing over the line.

Trey was waiting for them on the sidewalk outside the bar the following morning, a small duffel bag at his feet.

He didn't appear inclined to talk. Given Chase's concerns about the appropriate treatment of an amnesiac, Raine wasn't inclined to question him although there was so much she wanted to know. As a result, the drive home was spent listening to Chase's collection of CDs.

"Do you want me to drop you at the Saloon and Trey's apartment, or at your house?" Chase asked as they drove through the outskirts of Wolf Creek.

"My house, I think," Raine answered. "I can drop my bag and pick up my car, then drive Trey downtown to the apartment."

"Do whatever's most convenient." Trey spoke from the backseat where Killer kept him company. "And don't worry about me, Raine. I'm not ill, I just can't remember some things."

Raine wanted to argue with him but she knew he was right. "Sorry, Trey. Now that you're back, I don't want to let you out of my sight. I know I'm being irrational—I'm sure the feeling will go away after you've been home for a while."

"Makes sense," he responded.

"I promise I'll try very hard not to hover," she assured him.

Both Chase and Raine accompanied Trey up the back stairs to his apartment above the Saloon. Trey dropped his duffel on the sofa and turned in a slow circle.

"Does it seem familiar?" Raine asked, hoping he'd sensed a connection to the rooms.

"You know," he said slowly, studying the kitchen with its gleaming copper pans. "It does."

She felt a surge of relief. "Maybe your memory will return faster now that you're home, among friends and your own things."

"It can't be too soon for me. I'm damned tired of surprises," Trey said with feeling.

"Maybe we should let you settle in on your own," Chase said.

"Yes," Raine agreed. "That's probably a good idea. I'll see you later this afternoon, Trey?"

"Sure." He returned her hug with more ease than the day before.

"I need a few minutes to talk to Trey, Raine." Chase walked her out of the apartment and handed her his car keys. "I'll meet you downstairs."

"Is something wrong?"

"No." He bent his head and pressed a brief, warm kiss against her mouth. "I'll be down in a minute."

She nodded and left him.

Chase waited until she reached the bottom of the stairs before he re-entered the apartment. Arms crossed over his chest, Trey leaned against the countertop dividing the kitchen from the living room, his expression guarded.

"The sheriff's office ID'ed Carl and Bobby Rimes from the fingerprints in your vehicle," Chase said without preamble. "They've both disappeared and the sheriff believes they know they're wanted for questioning. I need your help to keep Raine safe while I track them down and bring them in."

Trey's face hardened. "You've got it. I don't remember the two—who are they?"

"Carl and Bobby are local brothers in their mid-thirties. They've been in and out of jail on minor crime convictions since they were teenagers. They've been working as hired hands at Harlan Kerrigan's ranch for the last ten months."

"Kerrigan?" Trey said slowly, frowning. "The name's familiar."

"It should be." Chase gave Trey a brief picture of the Kerrigan-McCloud-Harper connection. "I can't tell Raine about the Rimes brothers. If I do, she'll insist on going with me and when I refuse, she'll go looking on her own. This isn't like searching for you; this is dangerous. I don't want her hurt."

"Neither do I."

"Then I need your help. An agent with my company is on his way to guard Raine; he'll be here tonight. It should be easy enough for you to convince Raine you need her close to help you adjust to being back at the Saloon."

"I can do that," Trey agreed. "But how are you going to convince her not to go looking for the Rimes brothers? And won't she wonder where you are?"

"I'm going to lie to her," Chase said grimly.

"You mean about the Rimes brothers being involved?"

"Yeah. And about ending what's between us. I figure she'll be so mad at me, she won't want to see me for a while. She's too smart not to figure out something's going on if I just leave town and I can't guarantee I can always check in by phone. Plus I'd have to lie to her every time I was able to call her and increase the likelihood of her knowing something was wrong."

"You sure you want to do this?" Trey said dubiously. "Not that you don't need to tell her something to keep her from following you. I don't remember every-thing about my sister, but what I do know is that she's a smart, stubborn woman and she hates being lied to."

"I can't think of a better solution," Chase said, knowing Trey was right about Raine. If she didn't forgive him, he would lose her. "I won't risk her life. Will you help me?"

"Absolutely. But I'm not the one she's going to be mad at when she learns the truth. Not that she won't yell at me, but you're the one who's going to catch the most heat."

"I know." He took a slip of paper from his shirt pocket. "This is the cell phone number for Andy Jones, the Agency bodyguard. If you don't hear from him by five o'clock, call him. He'll watch her house but if you need him elsewhere, just tell him where and when."

"Chase."

He halted with his hand on the doorknob to look back at Trey.

"Just so we're clear—what exactly are your intentions toward my sister?"

"I plan to ask her to marry me just as soon as this is finished."

Trey grinned. "That's what I thought. Good luck."

Raine was quiet on the drive across town and so was Chase. Neither spoke as he followed her inside.

"Are you going to work today?" he asked, tucking a strand of hair behind her ear, his fingers gentle.

She nodded. "I told Trey I'd meet him in an hour to walk him through the Saloon and restaurant. We'll both explain to the staff what happened. It seems hard to believe, but I can get back to my normal routine now. Thanks to you." She stepped nearer, slid her arms around his neck and kissed him.

When he lifted his head, both were breathing faster. Raine reveled in the simmering sexual intensity that always flared when they touched.

"I'd better get going." He brushed the

corners of her mouth with kisses and stepped back.

"Will I see you tonight?" she asked.

"No."

Raine stared at him, the stark word and grim set of his mouth were a sharp contrast to the heated kiss they'd just shared.

"Tomorrow night?"

"No."

"Why am I getting the feeling you're trying to tell me something?" she asked, cold premonition skittering up her spine.

"The case is finished," he said, voice flat. "Trey's home. You're happy. End of story."

"End of story," she repeated slowly, trying to read his expression and failing. "And what about us?"

"There is no us. Your life is filled with running your businesses and your customers in Wolf Creek—you couldn't have one without the other. I wouldn't ask you to give that up and I'll never live in Wolf Creek, nor associate with the people here. We're as far apart as two people can get.

I don't see that changing." His voice lowered, turning raspy with emotion.

"Why does one of us have to give up our way of life for the other? Why can't we compromise?"

"I can't see a compromise that has a chance in hell of working." His eyes were remote.

"Can't we talk about this?" she said, desperate to reach him.

"Where would talking get us? We are who we are."

"People can change!"

"Maybe some people can," he said. "People without our history, maybe. But I don't see it happening for us."

"So that's it? You're just going to walk away?"

"I don't see an alternative."

"So, it was all a lie. I never meant more to you than good sex." Her pain threatened to consume her.

He reached her in one stride, grabbed her arms and took her mouth with so much carnal heat it burned away the chill of his words.

When he set her back on her feet, she swayed, disoriented.

"You were a hell of a lot more than great sex," he ground out.

Then he spun on his heel and left, leaving her with tears streaming down her face.

He doesn't love me. Each word was a hammer, causing fresh pain and tears. *If he did, he'd stay. We'd find a way to work this out.*

Fresh tears welled. She'd cried rivers of tears
 when Trey disappeared and thought nothing could ever hurt more. She hadn't known that finding Trey would mean losing Chase, nor that a heart could literally break.

Now she knew why she'd instinctively avoided relationships and falling in love before Chase. The pain of goodbye was equal to the depth of the love.

A mathematical equation.
Just her luck.
She'd never been good at math.

Chapter Ten

Raine could hardly believe Chase was
serious. Surely he wouldn't walk away
from her simply because she was tied to
Wolf Creek through her business interests?
She didn't care if he didn't want to interact
with the town residents—they'd find a way
to merge their lives. Couldn't they?

Clearly Chase didn't think so.

She had to face the possibility that
maybe she'd been the only one in love.

She carried a tray of ice cubes upstairs

to her bathroom and dumped them in the sink. Then she ran cold water over them, soaked a washcloth in the chilled water and held it to her eyes.

One look in the mirror told her it was going to take more than a few minutes and some ice cubes to erase the signs of her crying.

"Ugh. Men," she muttered, swishing the cloth in the cold water once again. After another ten minutes, she scrubbed her face, smoothed on moisturizer and carefully reapplied her makeup.

A half hour later, she walked up the back stairwell and knocked on Trey's door.

"Hi, come on in."

"I see you've decided to keep the beard," she said, studying his damp hair. He'd changed into a long-sleeved cotton shirt and rolled the cuffs back to just below his elbows. The pale blue checked cotton was tucked into the waistband of clean, faded jeans, a black leather belt with a dull silver buckle threaded through the belt loops. "Except for the stubble, you're looking more like the Trey I know," she commented, heading for the kitchen.

"Yeah." He dropped onto the sofa and pulled on his boots. "I've gotten used to it."

"Maybe the girls will think it's sexy," she teased. "Did you make coffee?"

"It's in the carafe."

Raine poured a mug, took a sip, and sighed. "Ah, now I *know* you're my Trey. Nobody makes coffee quite like you do."

"We can add that to the list of things I remember how to do," he said dryly. He crossed the room to pick up his own mug, sitting on the counter stool across from her. "I'm remembering more all the time. Details about my life—this kitchen, for instance." He gestured at the copper pans and chef stove. "I'm a damn good cook, right?"

"Yes," she laughed. "You're a fabulous cook."

He drained his mug and went into the

kitchen, rinsing it before slotting it into the dishwasher.

"I'll carry mine downstairs," she told him. "I hate to admit it, but the restaurant coffee hasn't been the same without you there to supervise."

"We'll take care of that," he promised with a grin.

"Excellent. My stomach thanks you. Are you ready to go downstairs?"

"Sure. We'll play this by ear, okay? I don't know how much I'll remember. I'm not worried about the work itself since I've been running the bar for Lori in Granger. But I don't know if I'll remember the people and I'd just as soon keep the extent of my memory loss as quiet as possible."

"Of course. We'll need to take Sam and Charlotte into our confidence but beyond the four of us, no one else needs to know." She paused, considering. "I'm sure you'll need to talk to the sheriff about what happened and the *Tribune* is sure to send a reporter to interview you."

"I don't mind filling out a report and telling the sheriff everything I can remember. But the reporter might be a problem."

"I'll sit in on the interview, if you'd like, and hopefully, between the two of us we can give them enough info to run a story but not enough for the paper to know about the amnesia."

"Sounds like a plan. And who are Sam and Charlotte?"

"Charlotte is the assistant manager of the restaurant and Sam has worked for us for years, since before Mom and Dad passed away."

"I remembered that earlier—about Mom and Dad, and Mike—when I was looking at framed photographs on the wall in the bedroom." His face was somber.

"There are a few things I wish you didn't have to remember, Trey. Our lives haven't always been filled with happiness."

He nodded and they left the apartment for the Saloon.

It was nearly empty. Sam was at the near end of the bar, his back to them.

"Sam," Raine said softly.

He turned, a broad smile on his face. "Raine, I didn't know you were home. Did you find any new information at the—" He broke off, shock erasing his smile as he caught sight of Trey.

"Hello, Sam." Trey closed the distance between them and the older man gave him a short hug.

"I'll be damned. I hardly recognized you with the beard." Sam's eyes were suspiciously bright. "Where the hell have you been?"

"It's a long story," Raine said. "Why don't you have Sheila take over for you and come into the office? I'll grab Charlotte from the restaurant so Trey only has to tell his story once."

"I'll be right there," Sam said. "Sheila's taking a coffee break next door."

"I'll send her over when I get Charlotte," Raine promised.

Charlotte was every bit as shocked and

delighted at seeing Trey as Sam had been. The four went into the office and spent the rest of the afternoon discussing strategy to handle Trey's return to the very public workplace. Since so many customers knew him, it wouldn't be easy to keep his memory lapses under wraps.

Chase spoke to Steve Blake at the sheriff's office for the latest update on the Rimes brothers' whereabouts before stopping at Luke's ranch to tell his brother where he was going.

"Trey doesn't know who robbed him and took his car?" Luke asked after hearing an abbreviated recitation of the events over the last few days.

"He can't remember the actual attack. He did say more memories about Wolf Creek are returning, but the week prior to his waking up in the ditch is still a blank."

"What about the letter?"

Chase shook his head. "A dead end."

"Trey didn't have it with him?"

"He has it," Chase said. "But the

address is illegible, water in the ditch left nothing but a few smears of blue ink on the envelope. The only clue is the Granger postmark."

"Damn." Luke slammed his palm against the corral post. "I was hoping we'd finally get lucky."

"Me, too." Chase shrugged. "I read the letter. It was short and cryptic with no solid information. It's possible the writer doesn't know anything and was running a scam to lure Trey into handing over money for non-existent evidence."

"I suppose it's too late to run the envelope and letter for possible finger-prints," Luke said morosely.

"Way too late." Chase glanced at his watch "I've got to get going. Don't forget to tell Dad and Mom I'm working on a case out of town. And give Trey and Andy a call today, let them know you're available if they need help."

"Stay in touch," Luke called after him as Chase climbed into his SUV.

The Rimes brothers had last been seen

in a small town on the outskirts of the Dakota Badlands. Chase drove south out of Wolf Creek to pick up their trail.

He tried to blank out the memory of Raine's tears but guilt rode him hard, shortening his temper. Each night he lay awake, missing her and unable to sleep while he fought the need to call her and explain. He knew he couldn't tell her the truth until the Rimes brothers were in custody and Harlan contained.

He hoped to God she'd forgive him.

After a frustrating week, Chase hit a dead end in Sioux Falls, South Dakota. The airport ticket agent remembered Carl and Bobby because the brothers had paid cash for two one-way tickets to Belize.

Chase didn't bother following them. He knew from past experience that a man on the run could easily lose himself in the Belize jungle or among the many cays just off the coast in the Gulf of Mexico.

He took the freeway on-ramp, leaving

Sioux Falls for Montana, and dialed Ren's cell phone.

"Where are you?" Ren demanded.

"On my way home," Chase said. "The Rimes brothers skipped to Belize. Have you found anything on Harlan?"

"Oh, yeah," Ren drawled. "Apparently, Mr. Kerrigan has a helluva social life in the capital city. Seems he's been sleeping with married women. Two of them have very rich and influential husbands. I suspect he's also involved in semi-legal business dealings but haven't had time to verify the rumors."

"It's about time we caught a break," Chase said with satisfaction "Where are you?"

"Helena."

"Good, I'll be there as soon as I can."

"I'm staying at the Hilton, room 324."

Chase hung up. He considered calling Raine but in the end, decided only a personal, face-to-face explanation would do and that would have to wait until after he and Ren were finished in Helena.

* * *

The restaurant was short a waitress and Raine took over setting tables, freeing the busboys to help the other waitresses. With efficient, practiced movements, she stripped a white tablecloth off a window table and replaced it. Napkins were ready with a few deft folds and heavy silverware completed the arrangement. She carried the used tablecloth to the utility room off the kitchen and dropped it in the dirty laundry.

Trey poked his head around the door. "Do you have a minute, Raine?"

"Of course."

"Let's go in the office."

Concerned, Raine followed him down the hall and into the office. "Is something wrong?"

He sat on the edge of the desk, one foot braced on the floor. "I remembered something this morning that might be important. Unfortunately, I'm sure it's not enough to get the sheriff involved."

"What is it?" Raine asked, dropping into the leather armchair facing the desk.

"More details about being carjacked. The two men who stopped when I was changing the flat tire were men I'd seen earlier at the accident scene. They were a couple of cars behind me, waiting for the state trooper to have the semi towed and clear the highway. We were all in the motel office at the same time, getting coffee from the desk clerk."

"Did they seem suspicious? Did you have any inkling they might try to rob you?"

"No." He shook his head. "They looked like ordinary cowboys after a day at work—dirty boots and jeans, beard stubble."

"But you'd recognize them if you saw them again?" Raine hoped so—she wanted the men who'd hurt Trey arrested, brought to trial and locked away in jail.

"I'm sure I would," Trey confirmed. "After they threw me in the back of my

SUV, I must have drifted in and out of consciousness a few times, because I remember bits and pieces of conversation. Most of it wasn't memorable but one of them mentioned Lonnie Kerrigan."

Raine tensed. "You're kidding."

"No, I'm not," he said grimly. "I don't have any proof, but I'm willing to bet Lonnie was connected with those two."

"Do you think Lonnie was involved somehow with the carjacking? But why?" Raine pushed upright, unable to sit still, and paced across the floor. "He's an obnoxious jerk but why would he want to have you robbed?"

Trey shrugged. "I have no idea. Nothing about my being carjacked makes sense. Why didn't they leave me along the road where they robbed me instead of driving a hundred miles away and throwing me in a ditch? And they could have killed me but they didn't. Of course, they might have assumed I'd die before anyone found me. I'm guessing I looked pretty bad when they dumped me out."

Raine winced. "I hope the police find them, soon, and lock them away for good."

"I'm more concerned about Lonnie Kerrigan," Trey said. "Did he or Harlan approach you or threaten you in any way?"

"Interesting you should ask," Raine said slowly. "I rarely have dealings with either of them but Harlan dropped by the office and Lonnie came into the Saloon one night. Both of them made veiled threats about my hiring Chase to look for you."

"What about since I've been home?"

She shook her head. "I haven't seen or talked to either of them recently."

"If you do hear from them, if they so much as say hello if you see them on the sidewalk, I want to know about it. In fact, I think I'll pay a call on the Kerrigans and tell them to stay away from you."

Something in Trey's expression reminded Raine of the edgy, dangerous warrior she'd glimpsed in Chase.

"Maybe we should talk to the McClouds first. I'm not saying you shouldn't talk to Harlan and Lonnie," she added quickly when he seemed about to disagree. "But if the Kerrigans are connected to you being attacked, then maybe it has something to do with the letter you received."

"Maybe." He stood. "I have to relieve Sam behind the bar. I'll think about waiting until I can talk to Chase."

Jessie walked into the restaurant just before noon. She waved at Raine and beckoned her closer.

"Can you join me for lunch?" she asked when Raine reached her.

"Of course." Raine took menus from the waitress. "Follow me, there's a table free near the window."

Jessie waited until they were seated before she spoke. "Dad's barbecuing this Sunday and Mom wants you to bring Trey and join us."

An invitation was the last thing Raine had expected. "It's lovely of her to invite us, Jessie, but I'm not sure we can make it."

Jessie eyed her shrewdly. "Chase won't be there, in case you're worried about running into him."

"I see. Is he out of town again?" *Maybe that's why I haven't heard from him,* she thought.

"He's working on a case—I only know because he told Luke, and Luke told Mom, who told me. Chase hasn't called anyone for days and he doesn't answer the phone or return messages." Jessie smiled her thanks at the waitress for the tall glass of iced tea and stirred in some sugar. "But you've talked to him, of course."

"No, I haven't."

"He hasn't called you, either?" Jessie grimaced in disgust. "I thought he must have told you what he was doing."

"I'm afraid your brother and I..." Raine paused, searching for the right words. "It's not likely he'll be calling me."

Jessie stared at her, clearly astonished. "But I was so sure after I saw the two of you together at the wedding... He did something stupid, didn't he? What was it? You can tell me," she said over Raine's halfhearted attempt to protest. "If there's one thing I know about my brothers, it's how impossible they can be. I've never met two more stubborn people in my life."

Raine had to grin at Jessie's annoyed expression. "Maybe it's brothers in general, or men in general, because Trey has times when he's beyond stubborn. And difficult. Let's not forget difficult."

"So, what did Chase do? Or say?"

"I believe he has issues with living in Wolf Creek," Raine said finally, trying to be diplomatic.

"Oh. That." Jessie sipped her tea and looked thoughtful. "I'd hoped he might be getting past those...issues."

"Apparently not."

"I wish I had a solution, Raine, but there are some things Chase refuses to discuss and interacting with the folks here in town is one of them."

"I know." Raine sighed. "Ah, well." She managed a small smile. "I'll always be thankful he helped me find Trey."

Their conversation turned to other subjects as Jessie ate her luncheon salad. She'd just finished when she glanced at her watch and gasped. "My goodness, look at the time. I have to run. I have an appointment at one. Promise you'll come out to the house on Sunday. Chase won't be there and we'd love to have you."

"I'll talk to Trey. If he can get away, we'll be there."

"Great." She glanced at the check, dropped several bills on top of it and stood. "Gotta run—see you Sunday."

And she was gone.

Now I understand why Zach fell in love with her, Raine thought. Chase's sister was smart and funny—Raine thought they might be friends, if only Chase wasn't her brother.

If Trey agreed, they'd go to the barbecue—it would give them an opportunity to tell the McClouds in a private setting about the possibility the Kerrigans were up to no good. But after

Sunday, it wasn't likely she'd see Jessie, or any of the McClouds often.

Raine wasn't ready to deal with social occasions that included Chase. She couldn't pretend he was only a friend.

Much to Raine's relief, her plan to use the barbecue get-together to tell the McClouds about Trey overhearing the carjackers worked just as she'd hoped.

And Chase hadn't appeared, just as Jessie had promised.

Raine was convinced Luke would waste no time telling his brother. She knew if anyone could make use of the information, it would be Chase.

While Raine and Trey were saying good-night to the McCloud clan, Chase and Ren were being ushered into the plush town home of Madelaine Harris, wife of the state senator Bill Harris.

"Good evening, gentlemen. Please," she gestured toward two armchairs facing the divan where she sat. "Have a seat."

"Thank you for agreeing to talk to us, Mrs. Harris." Chase took the chair nearest the silver-haired woman.

"You're welcome, Chase." She leaned forward, her eyes twinkling, and lowered her voice. "Don't tell my husband we had this conversation. He doesn't like Harlan Kerrigan any more than I do but unlike me, he has to work with him on occasion. Politics make strange bedfellows."

"We won't tell a soul where we got the information," Chase assured her.

"Excellent." She opened a drawer in the mahogany end table next to the divan and removed a folder, handing it to Chase. "When you called me, I knew I might have what you're looking for. These photos were given to me by a young woman whom Harlan seduced and them dumped. I gathered from her comments that he ended the relationship with an appalling lack of kindness. She was so outraged that she recruited her brother to follow Harlan and confirm her suspicions he was involved with another woman. The brother took the photos."

"How did you get them?" Chase asked, flipping through the six glossy 8x10's before passing them on to Ren. Handwritten names and dates were scribbled on the back of each print. The envelope also held the negatives.

"The young woman is the daughter of a friend of mine. She couldn't bring herself to use them against Harlan; I suspect she still harbors feelings for him, despite his treating her so badly. She came to me in hopes the photos might be useful if my husband reached an impasse with Harlan on a capitol construction project they're working on." She eyed Chase shrewdly. "I think perhaps they may be better used by you."

"Who's the woman in the photos?" Ren asked.

"She's the wife of a junior legislator from a mid-central voting district. Her husband ran on a moral values platform;

I'm certain he'd be very unhappy if those photos were made public."

"Not to mention what he'd do to Harlan," Chase said when he realized which well-known state legislator was married to the naked blonde in the picture.

"Ah, yes." Mrs. Harris's blue eyes twinkled with amusement. "That's the part of this scenario I thought might aid you."

"It does." Chase stood and bent to kiss her cheek. "Thank you."

"You're most welcome. Tell your mother hello for me, will you."

They were outside on the sidewalk before Ren spoke.

"You've got friends in the right places, McCloud. How did you know she'd have something on Kerrigan?"

"Madelaine Harris has been around politics since she was a baby—her father was a senator—and she married a successful politician. If skeletons are hanging in anyone's closet, Maddy knows about them. I should have told you to contact her but I didn't think of it until I drove into town."

"Are the photos enough for you to talk to Harlan?" Ren asked as they fastened their seat belts and left the upscale neighborhood.

"Oh, yeah," Chase said with satisfaction. "I'd like you to stay here and follow up on the construction project in the morning, see if you can find any proof Harlan's bribing legislators to get it passed. I'll go home and have a talk with Harlan. After that I'll check in with Trey and Andy to let them know they're officially relieved of guard duty."

Then I can talk to Raine. Finally.

He hoped she'd listen.

And then forgive him for lying to her.

The following evening, Raine closed up the restaurant, then walked down the hall to say good night to Trey.

But the bartender wasn't Trey. Raine swept the room, quickly eliminating the Monday-night crowd.

"Kelly, where's Trey?" She raised her voice to be heard above the jukebox.

"He went upstairs—said to tell you he's tired and he'll call you later."

Raine knew Trey hadn't slept well the night before so she merely nodded, slung her purse over her shoulder and headed for the door. She sidestepped a boisterous couple trying to dance and was only a few feet from the exit when Chase entered.

Raine stopped abruptly. She wanted to walk closer until she could put her arms around him, feel him hold her in return, breathe in the mix of soap, leather and man that was uniquely Chase.

The thought that she didn't have the right to do so broke her heart.

She steeled herself against the pain and the tears that choked and burned in the back of her throat, sheer will keeping her in place. She was afraid to speak for fear her voice would break.

Chase stared back at her, the only evidence of emotion a muscle that flexed along his jawline.

"I'm looking for Trey," he said finally.

"He's upstairs."

"Thanks." He eyed her moodily. "Raine…"

"Kelly said Trey left early because he was tired," she broke in, afraid Chase was about to tell her he was sorry. She couldn't bear to hear him apologize for not being able to love her. "Don't keep him up too late."

She brushed by him and left the Saloon, not looking back.

An hour later, she lay in bed, unable to sleep. She tossed back the covers and padded out of her bedroom. She was halfway down the stairs when the doorbell rang.

"It's nearly midnight—who can that be?" she murmured, hurrying the rest of the way down the stairs.

A quick check through the window drapes revealed the tall, broad shape of a man. A man she recognized instantly.

She bit her lip, hesitating before

switching on a lamp and letting him in. "What are you doing here?"

"We need to talk."

Raine crossed her arms and sat on the arm of the sofa. "Did you see Trey?"

"Yeah, I talked to him. Why didn't you tell me as soon as you knew about the carjackers using Lonnie's name?"

"We told Luke—I knew he'd tell you."

"You promised me you'd come to me if Lonnie bothered you again."

"He hasn't been near me," she protested. "I heard Harlan sent him back to Helena after he was arrested for fighting with you at the Saloon."

"Just because he's out of town doesn't mean he can't stir up trouble." Chase stepped closer, until his legs bumped her knees and she had to tip her head back to look up at him. "I don't like you being alone here."

"I feel perfectly safe, Chase." Raine couldn't bear being so close to him. She slid sideways and off the sofa, moving several steps away.

He took a step toward her. "I need to explain—about Harlan and…other things."

She took a step back. "Never mind. I don't want to hear and I'd like you to leave. It's late and I have to work tomorrow."

He stared at her, his frustration palpable. "I know you don't want to listen, Raine, but I need to tell you."

"I thought you said you didn't want to see me again. I assumed that meant we wouldn't be talking."

"Hell." He thrust his fingers through his hair. "I knew you wouldn't make this easy. I lied to you when I told you I didn't want to see you again," he said. "I'm sorry and I wish I hadn't had to do it but I couldn't think of any other way to keep you from following me. And it was too damned dangerous to have you along."

"Following you?" she said, stunned. "Where?"

"The two men who carjacked Trey were Carl and Bobby Rimes. The sheriff identified them by the fingerprints they left in Trey's SUV. I tracked them to South Dakota and lost them when they boarded a flight to Belize.

"Then I went to Helena," he continued when she was too speechless to respond, "where Ren and I uncovered information about an affair Harlan's been having with a politician's wife. I paid a visit to Harlan today, gave him copies of the photos, and told him if he so much as said hello to either you or Trey in the future, I'd send the originals to the newspapers. I don't think we need to worry about him or Lonnie bothering you again."

Raine felt her eyes widen in shock.

"I know," Chase said with a wry grin. "Blackmail isn't the method I would have chosen to control him, but at the moment, it's the best I've got." His expression turned sober. "I want you safe, Raine. And I don't trust Harlan. If he was connected to Trey's carjacking, then you're in danger, too. It was sheer chance you weren't in the car with Trey that night."

He reached her in one long stride and cupped her shoulders in his hands. "I'll do whatever's necessary to keep you safe. I never thought I'd feel this way about anyone. I love you. I want to marry you, if you'll have me."

Raine couldn't speak past the rush of tears. She slipped her arms around his waist and buried her face against his shirt.

"I'm hoping you're crying because you're happy."

"I'm happy," she whispered.

"Forgive me?" he murmured, tipping her face up to his.

"Yes, but I reserve the right to yell at you tomorrow."

"Absolutely, tomorrow is good. Tomorrow is much better than tonight." He brushed kisses against the corners of her mouth and down her throat. "I haven't seen you naked in days," he murmured, his voice full of emotion. "Let's go to bed."

"Yes, let's," she breathed, her skin

blooming with heat where his mouth and hands touched and stroked.

He bent and slipped an arm under her knees, swinging her off her feet. She linked her arms around his neck and nuzzled his throat.

"You are going to say yes, aren't you?" he said.

"Of course," she said. "What was the question?"

"Will you marry me?"

Her arms tightened and she leaned back to look up at him. "Will you settle down and make a home with me here? Can you promise me you won't spend the rest of your life searching for a way to prove Harlan set you up when Mike died?"

"Don't you want to know what happened that night?"

"Yes. But I want closure. I want to share my life with someone focused on our future, not on the past." She waited for his answer, watching the struggle of emotions on his face.

"I want that, too," he said at last, "and

I'm willing to do whatever it takes to make it happen."

Raine could breathe again. "Can we have babies?" she teased softly, her heart soaring with happiness.

"All you want."

"Good. Then I'm definitely going to say yes."

"You won't be sorry," he vowed. He dropped her onto the bed and followed her down. Nudging his leg between hers, he covered her mouth and body with his.

Chase surveyed the neatly cut grass and the square plot of bright wildflowers around the base of the gray headstone. "It's nice here, calm and peaceful."

Raine slipped her arm through his. "Have you visited the cemetery since you moved back home?"

"A few times. I brought flowers to Granddad's grave."

"The bouquet of roses I found here a few months ago—they were from your mother's garden, weren't they."

"Yes."

"I wondered who'd left them. Thank you," she said softly.

He covered her hand with his and pressed a kiss against her temple. "You're welcome."

"We were here, you know," Trey put in. "Up there." He gestured toward the hill. "The day your grandfather Angus was buried."

"No wonder I didn't see you," Chase said.

"Did you look for us?" Raine said.

"I didn't expect you to be there, but yes, I looked."

"Mom would have been furious if she'd known we were here. We knew the gossips were sure to tell her." Raine looked at the hill, feeling the wind and cold chill of that long-ago day. "So we hid behind a sagebrush. I'm sorry we couldn't let you know," she murmured.

"You two said you had a specific reason for asking me to meet you out here today." Trey said, changing the subject. "Not that I mind visiting Mike." He laid his palm on the waist-high granite marker. "But I'm curious."

"I asked Raine to marry me last night," Chase said. "And she said yes, if I could let go of the past. As of today, I'll stop searching for whoever wrote the letter you received. I'm going to concentrate on being her husband and hopefully, someday a father to our children. We thought it was fitting to tell Mike—" He paused to clear his throat before continuing. "To tell Mike what we're doing, and why, and ask for his blessing."

"You can't be serious." Disbelief vibrated in Trey's words. "You're really going to leave it like this? Just turn your back and walk away—never follow up on the only clue that might uncover what really happened to Mike?"

"I'm not saying I've forgotten how Mike died that night, nor that I wouldn't like to see Lonnie brought to justice. But I want a life with Raine more." Chase's voice rang with quiet conviction. "You need to let it go too, Trey. Mike wouldn't want you to waste your life searching for proof that might not even exist."

"We want your blessing, too, Trey,"

Raine said, worried by his blank expression.

"You have it," he said. "Of all the people in the world, no one is more deserving of a chance to start married life free of old history."

Tears dampened Raine's face. "Thank you, Trey," she whispered.

Wordlessly, Chase handed her his handkerchief.

"I'm sure Mike would say the same." Trey left the granite marker and held out his arms.

Raine walked into them and he hugged her tight.

"Be happy," he whispered against her hair before he released her to Chase.

Later that evening, Raine lay in Chase's arms, naked and replete with bone-deep contentment.

"Do you think we convinced Trey this afternoon?"

"When I told him Mike would want him to move on with his life?" Chase asked, threading strands of her hair through his fingers.

She nodded, the movement tugging her hair from his loose grip.

"I'm not sure." He smoothed his palm over the inward curve of her waist before stroking the sensitive skin of her bottom. "I doubt it. He doesn't have the incentive I have."

"And that would be…?" she murmured.

He wrapped his arms around her and rolled, settling atop her, his weight holding her captive. "You." He brushed kisses against the corners of her mouth. "Let's get married tomorrow."

"Tomorrow?" Startled, she stared up at him. "We can't get married tomorrow!"

"Sure we can. Las Vegas is only a few hours away by plane."

"I want a wedding like your sister's."

He lifted his head, clearly surprised. "You do?"

"Until I met you, I hadn't really thought about having a grand wedding but now—" She trailed off, mulling over the idea. "I want to walk down the aisle and see you look at me the way Zach looked at Jessie."

"Honey, I look at you like that all the time," Chase said, his voice husky. "I'm crazy about you. Haven't you noticed?"

She had. She loved it. She loved him. And wonder of wonders, he loved her.

"I love you, too," she whispered, just before he kissed her and the world fell away.

* * * * *

Look for the fourth and final book in

THE McCLOUDS OF MONTANA
miniseries,

TREY'S SECRET

on sale April 2007
only from Silhouette Special Edition.

New York Times *bestselling author Linda Lael Miller is back with a new romance featuring the heartwarming McKettrick family from Silhouette Special Edition.*

SIERRA'S HOMECOMING
by Linda Lael Miller

On sale December 2006, wherever books are sold.

Turn the page for a sneak preview!

Soft, smoky music poured into the room.

The next thing she knew, Sierra was in Travis's arms, close against that chest she'd admired earlier, and they were slow dancing.

Why didn't she pull away?

"Relax," he said. His breath was warm in her hair.

She giggled, more nervous than amused. What was the matter with her? She was attracted to Travis, had been from the first, and he was clearly attracted to her. They were both adults. Why not enjoy a little slow dancing in a ranch-house kitchen?

Because slow dancing led to other things. She took a step back and felt the counter flush against her lower back. Travis naturally came with her, since they were holding hands and he had one arm around her waist.

Simple physics.

Then he kissed her.

Physics again—this time, not so simple.

"Yikes," she said, when their mouths parted.

He grinned. "Nobody's ever said that after I kissed them."

She felt the heat and substance of his body pressed against hers. "It's going to happen, isn't it?" she heard herself whisper.

"Yep," Travis answered.

"But not tonight," Sierra said on a sigh.

"Probably not," Travis agreed.

"When, then?"

He chuckled, gave her a slow, nibbling kiss. "Tomorrow morning," he said. "After you drop Liam off at school."

"Isn't that…a little…soon?"

"Not soon enough," Travis answered, his voice husky. "Not nearly soon enough."

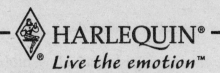
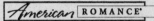

HARLEQUIN®

Super Romance®

...there's more to the story!

Superromance.
A *big* satisfying read about unforgettable
characters. Each month we offer *six* very different
stories that range from family drama to adventure
and mystery, from highly emotional stories to
romantic comedies—and much more! Stories
about people you'll believe in and care about.
Stories too compelling to put down....

Our authors are among today's *best* romance
writers. You'll find familiar names and talented
newcomers. Many of them are award winners—
and you'll see why!

If you want the biggest and best
in romance fiction, you'll get it
from Superromance!

Exciting, Emotional, Unexpected...

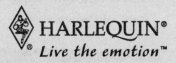

HARLEQUIN®
Live the emotion™